D0899514

# ONLY
# YOU

# ONLY YOU

## EROTIC ROMANCE
## FOR WOMEN

EDITED BY
RACHEL KRAMER BUSSEL

CLEiS
PRESS

Copyright © 2012 by Rachel Kramer Bussel.

All rights reserved. Except for brief passages quoted in newspaper, magazine, radio, television, or online reviews, no part of this book may be reproduced in any form or by any means, electronic or mechanical, including photocopying or recording, or by information storage or retrieval system, without permission in writing from the publisher.

Published in the United States by Cleis Press, Inc., 2246 Sixth Street, Berkeley, California 94710.

Printed in the United States.
Cover design: Scott Idleman/Blink
Cover photograph: Medioimages/Photodisc
Text design: Frank Wiedemann

First Edition.
10 9 8 7 6 5 4 3 2 1

Trade paper ISBN: 978-1-57344-909-0
E-book ISBN: 978-1-57344-922-9

# Contents

# INTRODUCTION: VERY HAPPY ENDINGS

Honey, are you happy?" is the question with which Cassandra Carr opens her story, "Saved," about a marriage that needs reviving, pronto. Haven't we all been in relationships where we longed to ask our partners what they were truly thinking and feeling; whether they were happy; whether they had fantasies, regrets, dreams—but didn't ask because we were afraid of the answer? I certainly have, so I have extra admiration for this lonely wife who dares to ask for what she wants, realizing it's never too late. That is the same spirit that enlivens every story in this collection, where sexual pleasure and romantic happiness are not guaranteed at the outset. Couples in various stages of their romances experience tricky territory and have to ask, pursue, explore and test the boundaries of their love in order to reach new peaks, learn about themselves, and make their relationships stronger. Yes, these stories are hot, and I fully encourage you to read them with one hand, but I also find them heartwarming. They explore what happens within a marriage or relationship behind closed doors, for the most part, when you're stripped bare in the literal and figurative senses, and are truly seen by someone who knows you inside and out.

You very likely know the feeling of being captivated by a lover, wanting to be with him morning, noon and night; dreaming about her when you're away; reveling in the heights of passion as well as the tender comforts of togetherness when you're not. The stories in *Only You* celebrate that feeling of knowing the ones you love for all their high points and their faults, of seeing beyond their outer image to what truly makes their heart beat, sometimes knowing them better than they know themselves.

The stories you are about to read all explore the theme, in some way, of lovers who are drawn to each other, whether they fully understand why or not. Some are pulled apart by obstacles they have to overcome, and others simply can't wait to tear each other's clothes off. Some serve as teachers, guides or gurus into matters of the heart.

What I especially like about these tales is that the lovers here join forces, using their knowledge of what the other person gets off on to spur them to risqué acts, even under circumstances that may not seem ideal at first glance. "Forgotten Bodies," by Giselle Renarde, addresses the ways we can forget our own bodies, not to mention our partner's libido, in long-term relationships. Susan goes so far as to hide in the bathroom to avoid sex with her husband, only to discover that he's cooking up something new and naughty for them to try. In "The Love We Make," by Kristina Wright, fighting leads to the hottest sex imaginable, and means there's no excuse too petty to pick a fight over, if they get to "make up." Sex-starved Sidney in Lolita Lopez's "Mom's Night Out" engages in a one-night getaway with her husband, Owen, where they forget all about the draining daily duties of parenthood and rediscover how much they still hunger for each other.

Some of the lovers here are less experienced, such as M. in "Autumn Rain," by Michael A. Gonzales, and Dean in my story "For the Very First Time." Each delicately touches on the ways our first time leaves an impression, makes us fall that much harder for the person we're sharing the momentous occasion with. Even when the characters aren't actually virginal, when they approach their relationships anew, finding something novel in their partner's kiss or touch, they can invoke Madonna and feel "Like a Virgin," only with the bonus of a shared, special history.

As I've edited this collection, I've been listening to Adele's achingly gorgeous album *21*. Those songs are about lost loves, but they contain all the tenderness you will find here as well, and rest assured, not to give too much away, the tales in *Only You* have happy, sweet, sexy endings.

I wish you *only* pleasure in enjoying the stories you're about to read.

Rachel Kramer Bussel
New York City

# DRIVEN

## Angela Caperton

Suzanne leaned back in the passenger seat and closed her eyes, letting the smooth hum of the road and Willie's easy croon on the satellite radio soothe her. Tom Blessington drove the Fit among a thin flow of cars and trucks on the four-lane state road that led from the park back to town. His right arm rested on the console between them, within easy reach of the gearshift and close enough to Suzanne's thigh that his body warmth seeped deliciously into her bones.

They had taken bikes out to the park and ridden all morning on the big loop that circled Lost Lake, pausing for a light brunch, sharing the silence of the cultivated wilderness on a weekday when most of the world was at work.

This was their second real date, Suzanne realized, after four lunches and pages of texts. Neither one of them were kids—Tom had just turned forty, and she was only three years younger. Life was too short for pretense, she often thought, and after the day they'd just shared, she was ready to go to bed with him.

She glanced at him with a soft smile. If he would let her know he wanted to as well, they'd enjoy the rest of the day tangled in sheets. Two years was too long to have gone without sex but, in that time, none of her flirtations or little courtships had progressed past dating. It wasn't that Suzanne was especially demanding, but most of the men she met seemed a little desperate or overly aggressive. Tom seemed right, and it was time to end the long dry spell. Her instincts hinted that Tom would be an attentive lover, if only he'd be a little bold and let her know he was interested. She wasn't looking for him to toss her on the ground and rip her clothes off, although at the moment, that didn't sound so bad. *Horny,* she told herself. *You're just fucking horny, Suzanne.*

Willie finished singing "Crazy" and Tom switched the station to jazz, something Suzanne didn't recognize but instantly liked. The music mirrored the weather, light and breezy. When his arm returned to the console, the back of his fingers brushed her thigh, just above the hem of her short skirt. On an impulse, she reached across and petted him, tracing his knuckles.

Her heart tripped at his response, a quiet shiver that she knew was not the vibration of the car. Air froze in her lungs as he turned his hand under her touch, their fingers not quite lacing. He gripped the wheel harder with his left hand and turned to look at her. An impish glee skipped in her belly, along with the certainty that this moment was the signal she'd been waiting for. Their gazes met and Suzanne knew he saw the mischief in her eyes, and she saw something in his, the crystal prism of challenge, and without hesitation, she raised his hand to her lips. With her heart beating a quickening rhythm, she kissed the center of his palm, the tip of her tongue swirling a clear invitation.

Tom drew a deep breath and caressed her cheek with his

fingers. He looked back and forth between her and the road, settling into the right lane far behind the nearest car. Holding his wrist, Suzanne guided his touch to the open neck of her cotton blouse and his warm hand took the hint, stroking her throat, his eyes full of questions every time he turned to look at her.

Suzanne matched the depth of his breathing with her own as she released his hand. He kept touching her, tracing the line of her jaw then down along her clavicle, each exploration shocking her nerves into a sultry dance. She began to unbutton her blouse and grinned as the car jerked ever so slightly. A truck passed on the left but she barely acknowledged the reality of it.

Beneath the white cotton, she wore a thin bra, translucent and flesh-toned. Her nipples had stiffened to peaks and the heat of his gaze, as she opened the last button and let the shirt fall open, emboldened her.

"What are you doing?" he asked with a nervous laugh.

"Mmm," she replied, and smiled at him, unwilling to instruct him, savoring her impulsiveness.

He slowed the Fit more, hanging at the bottom of the speed limit, and his hand moved apparently with a mind of its own, hot and eager to touch. He ran his fingers reverently over the point of her erect nipple, and warm silk flowed between her legs. Air pushed out of her lungs, edging toward panting, short, hard and fast as he circled the tip, and then her breathing bumped into ragged sighs as he slid his finger under the tight gauze of the bra. Rationality evaporated as she reached back, unfastened the bra, and let the satiny garment fall away, leaving her breasts bare to his touch, to his gaze—and the gaze of anyone casually driving by them. A thick, thermal fog hazed her brain as she slipped free of the passenger seat shoulder harness and shed both her blouse and the bra, tossing them into the backseat, out of reach.

"Watch the road," she teased as she noticed his obvious effort to keep them on course, but his eyes and his hand were pulled to her like iron filings to a magnet. Suzanne found the seat adjustment and reclined the seat. She stretched, reveling in the pure lust that boiled in her blood and that she saw mirrored in Tom's expression. The intoxicating thrill of being half naked in the front seat of his car infused her pussy with a keen throbbing ache of want. She had never ever done anything like this before, but the sultry heat of the car added to the pure brazenness of the act. Nothing had ever felt more sinfully right. If this wasn't enough to help Tom overcome his silly shyness, Suzanne would just have to declare him dead and move on.

Another car passed them and she saw the passenger's head move to look forward. Had he seen her? Suzanne just smiled. She had to admit, the thought that a passing stranger might have seen her bare breasts through the windows of the car thrilled her and added to the excitement of her display. The slick moisture between her legs became a trickle.

Tom's touch turned rougher as he palmed her breast and rolled the stiff nipple under his hand, the hard kneading adding an edge to her arousal. She gasped and arched; caught his wrist and urged his hand lower, down the flat plane of her stomach, still a little damp with sweat from the morning ride. His thumb hooked under the waistband of her skirt as she squirmed in the seat.

Tom's devilish grin gilded a glow to her growing lust. He looked more boyish than she had ever seen him, his cheeks coloring and his eyes wild with the promise of buried treasure.

She stroked the back of his hand, guided his touch with light pressure. She loosened her skirt to improve his access, and when his fingertips caressed the little fringe of hair above her pussy through the lacy thong she wore, she thought her heart might stop completely. Hungry for his touch, nearly crazed with desire, she eased herself up in the seat and shifted so his hand slid down until his fingers rested atop her clit.

Divinity illuminated her, wanton, pagan and wicked, as she celebrated her sexuality in the suspended warmth of the car, the road and wind percussion combining with the perfect Latin-jazz beat coming from the speakers. The world beyond the glass and metal melted into a matte of textured color, barely seen, hardly acknowledged. All that mattered was Tom, his hand between her legs, the steady thrum of the car he still managed to keep on the road, the ribbon of discovery as cars and trucks zoomed by them.

He pushed against the lace barrier that was fast soaking with her desire, and his fingers parted her, rubbing the silk of her sexual surrender between the lips. He found her clit with skilled fingers and Suzanne teetered on the edge of climax. Not enough. Not yet.

"Wait," she nearly groaned, then reached under her skirt, removed the thong and tossed it to join her blouse and bra. She bunched the soft linen skirt on her belly to show him what he wanted to see in the golden spotlight of sun through the windshield and windows. She opened to him, to the sky and the sun and the road.

"I'll pull over," he said.

She knew the road. There was nowhere close to pull off, no turnoff, no roadside park for miles. Tucking her skirt up, almost naked beside him, she made a sound that said, quite articulately, she had no intention of waiting.

The car accelerated as his hand found her bare pussy, his middle finger sliding perfectly over her clit, then into her. Her wetness ensured she hardly had to open to him, but she did, spreading her legs, her right knee pressed against the upholstered door interior, offering him as much access as he needed. Tom began to fuck her with his fingers: first one, then two, slipping, curling into the soaked slit; spreading her as he pumped, his palm massaging her clit. The slick sounds of his fingerfucking merged with the music and the keening of her breath as ripples of pleasure turned into waves. The first orgasm rose like a cork in water, an eruption from depths she had never known before. Head back, breasts out, pressed against the car seat, her pussy constricting around his relentless hand, she came hard, crying out. Merciless, Tom's fingers continued and, to Suzanne's amazement and delight, only a few more pumps produced another orgasm that rocked her body, seared her nerves and blinded her to everything but the ecstasy coursing through her. Shuddering, the road bright on her closed lids, nothing existed except his touch still coaxing and working inside her.

She reached across, breathless, and stroked his cock through his jeans, a solid rod of flesh that looked dangerously alive and painfully entrapped. He nodded, the sheen of animal desire glazing his eyes and dotting his forehead in sweat. She unzipped him, his hand losing its access as she twisted, the car slowing again.

Another semi-truck passed and honked its horn in two jubilant toots. Suzanne laughed, unabashed and giddy; she had no doubt that at least one trucker had seen them and enjoyed the show. Sated, but eager for Tom, she really didn't care who might be watching them. No rest or concern until the mission was complete.

Her fingers slipped inside the slit of his boxers and his cock popped effortlessly free of its confinement. Her smile stretched wide. His prick was every bit as perfect as she had hoped it would be—a good length and circumcised, silky veins, and thick, with a shining head crowned by a brilliant dribble of precome. She wanted him inside her, wanted to straddle him and let him fill her, but the Fit wasn't made for that, and she admitted the anticipation of his cock inside her rejuvenated her horniness. She stretched against the disjointed seat belt. Without a thought, she unfastened the restraint and tossed her last garment away. For a moment, she savored the freedom of complete nudity, hoping someone else would pass them. She imagined herself splaying her thighs and making rude gestures to any scowls of disapproval.

She knelt in the seat, leaned over the console and kissed the head of Tom's cock, smearing the precome, rolling the salty juice on her tongue. He tasted like sweat and musk, warm spice and heat. She wanted more.

Sunshine through the windshield heated her cheek as she took the stiff flesh into her mouth, her lips a tight O, her fingers stroking the pulsing base, teasing his balls. Her tongue cradled his cock as she slid her mouth over him, and pulling away, she let her tongue whip and play with the sensitive ridge and spongy head. Slow at first, her mouth learned his cock, her lips quickly mapped the throbbing veins, her tongue tasted the landscape of his skin. Delicious, hot, hard and hers, Suzanne savored his excitement and her rhythm grew. Tom's hand crowned her head, his fingers kneading her skull in sync with her mouth. She delighted at the momentary acceleration of the car when Tom tried to thrust up and his foot pressed on the gas.

"Suzanne..." he said, then growled like an alert mastiff as he stiffened behind the wheel, the car swerving a little as he came in hot, glorious spurts on her tongue and in her throat. She tithed his shrinking shaft one more lick and sat up. The bright, beautiful day bathed her and she stretched, entirely open and free to whatever might happen next. Tom looked at her with an expression of barely satisfied lust and she knew that, whenever they got to her place, they would find an entirely new level of pleasure together. She glanced at his cock and grinned to see it shiny with her saliva and already twitching with new life.

"Don't dress," he said, his hand on her thigh, fingers finding the folds of her pussy again.

"I have no intention of dressing," she said, watching the roadside.

"I'm not finished, and we've a long way to go," he said, his finger working her clit again.

"Don't worry," she said, her hand on his fingers as they teased her dripping lips. "You're driving and I'm not going anywhere without you."

# OVERCOME

## Alyssa Turner

It was dark, but his silhouette was unmistakable, square and lean a few feet away from her.

"How did you know I was here?" Riley chewed her lip, huddled against the arm of the raggedy couch, eyeing the duffel bag at Max's feet.

"Same way you knew I would come."

"You didn't have to," she whispered.

"The hell I didn't."

"You gonna turn me in?

"What do you think?" He bent down to remove a grease-stained package from the duffel. "Brought you a burger."

"Cheese?"

"Nah. I know you like cheese, but it was all they had at the gas station this time of night."

Riley twisted her mouth into a teasing smirk. "You're such a disappointment."

He returned her irony with a laugh, taking another step

forward and cracking a smile in the moonlight, making Riley wish she could throw her arms around him. Instead, she took the paper bag from his hand and set it on the coffee table amidst the dust and debris.

Headlights flashed into the room from the road. Hardly anyone ever drove so far off the highway that time of night. Her bare shoulders twitched as the high beams cut through the darkness.

Max still lingered at the edge of the couch, too far to reach her even if he wanted to. But the brief illumination gave him a glimpse of her face, stained in mascara, frightened.

"I'm in trouble, Max."

"I know, baby."

"Why didn't I listen to you?"

"You never did before," he chuffed. "Not one time in all the years we spent in this place. That hard head of yours...kept you in plenty of hot water with old Ms. Perry, too, remember?"

Ms. Perry hadn't let her foster children call her anything else. The word *mom* wasn't part of either of their vocabularies and the concept of family was as intangible as the grayed woman's constant plumes of smoke, blowing through the rooms like a ghost. The stench of cigarettes still clung to the wallpaper of the abandoned house more than eight years later.

Riley tried to explain. "Devon was just supposed to pick up some product from his dealer. That fucker didn't tell me he was going to rob the guy. He just dropped the gun and left me standing there! I called nine-one-one, Max, and I ran." She lowered her eyes. "Did he kill him? Big G—is he dead?"

"He got tagged in the shoulder; he'll live." Max took a seat on the other side of the tattered couch. "What the hell were you thinking getting mixed up with that lowlife?"

"Which one?"

He laughed. "Yeah right; you always had a talent for hooking up with the biggest asshole you could find."

"Not always," she whispered with unmistakable apology.

"P.O. Dwyer, respond." Max's radio raked the silence. "Dwyer."

Riley took a breath, holding it as Max lifted the radio from his duffel bag and she awaited his reply.

"Dwyer here, Sarge."

"Ten-five your location, officer."

Riley could sense his big blue eyes burning her face, staring through the darkness as he spoke. "Fifth and Burrow, couple of kids boozing it up."

Dwyer continued, "Suspect is in custody on that two-eleven. Unidentified Latino female twenty to twenty-five, five-six to five-eight, in a yellow top, white shorts is still wanted for questioning."

"Ten-four," Max responded and tossed the radio back into the bag.

"Latino? Try half-Irish, half-Jamaican," Riley said to the air and jumped off the couch. "I gotta get out of here. The cab driver will definitely remember me."

Max leaned forward and grabbed her arm, pulling her back down in front of him. She was shaking and he steadied her with his other hand on her cheek.

"Riley, why?"

She knew he wasn't talking about how she'd ended up on the eleven o'clock news, caught on surveillance entering G's apartment building with her latest bad decision. After they'd fooled around last year, why did she shut Max out? She had as little courage to explain that as any other asinine choice she'd made. Why? Fear was the plain answer—fear of hurting him, fear of not hurting herself for a change.

His thumb grazed slowly over the sharp bridge of her nose and across her eyebrow, then repeated the same worn path, something he'd done so many times before when Riley needed the reassurance of his touch. When they were kids, she'd come running to his bedroom in the middle of the night, tiptoeing across the bare planks of the old house and tapping their secret knock on his door. Nightmares plagued her routinely, but once she was cuddled up in his bed, Max had instinctually delivered those same caresses to stop her from trembling.

Now they made her weak. His closeness was painful, something she felt she didn't deserve, too good to be true. It took everything inside her to muster the willpower to push him away, but Max wouldn't stand for it. Not this time.

He slipped his fingers to the back of her head, weaving them into her dark, spiraling curls and brushed his lips against hers. She shuddered, wanting him more than ever. Opening her mouth, she dared to taste happiness for just the smallest moment. His tongue was deliciously complicit, erasing the worry from her face. Truth flowed from his tender kiss. He belonged to her.

"Max, no..."

"Stop, Riley. Stop making this so hard."

"You don't want me. I'm all fucked up." Tears pooled and threatened to overflow.

"I know." He sucked softly on her neck, speaking against her skin. "You've always been fucked up." His hand fell to her shoulder, fingers slinking under her spaghetti strap and tugging the yellow strip of fabric away. "And I've always loved you anyway."

"Don't say that, Max."

His eyes were closed and his chest heaved, inhaling her. "Just shut up already," he breathed, finding her lips again and cloaking her in his arms.

How could she resist such comfort? The fight exhausted her, and she was already so weary. She let herself melt against him, the strength of his heartbeat bumping her chest. This was so much more real than the daydreams she tried not to let tickle her hopes. That was a losing battle; he was always in the back of her mind.

Riley slipped her arms around his waist, maneuvering over the gun protruding from his side. After four years on the job, Max was plainclothes most of the time now, but the standard gun belt still applied. He took his arms away to remove it and drop it onto the bag, but didn't let his tongue stop dancing with hers for a second.

Riley was grateful; she never wanted him to stop. *One last time, and then I'll let him go.*

The couch meant only for the good company that never came creaked under their weight as Max pressed forward. His mouth hungered for her response, desperate to feel her need him in return, and she relented under the magnitude of it, his need and hers. In the firm sweeps of his tongue, he tried to own her, even though it was clear he never would, not entirely. The chase kept him coming back.

Somewhere inside Riley knew this, and she wondered, if she ever stopped running would he be content to have her? She reached instinctually for his cock, curious to know how much he wanted her right then.

The mere touch of her hand massaging his length was enough to make him moan. Max wasn't exactly celibate. Still, the slapping of unfamiliar flesh in the wee hours of loneliness wasn't making love—not the love he wanted to make to her. But the setting was all wrong, and the timing was worse.

Max pulled away. "We need to get on the road. I want to get to the border before daybreak."

Riley was disappointed, but kept her tone even. "The border?"

"You have your ID, don't you?"

"Yes, but—"

"I told you I'd always look out for you, Riley. And I meant it, even though you're good at making it damn near impossible." He opened the duffel bag again to pull out a pink T-shirt and black leggings, the tags still on. "Here, change your clothes first. Your description's been blasted to every police station for a hundred miles."

"Pink!" Riley frowned.

"You wanna stop busting my balls?" He grinned, white teeth breaking out on his shadowed face.

"Never." In this room, their playful banter was more than familiar. It was almost like home.

"I hope you mean that," he said, more serious than she'd like.

It would be so easy if she weren't such a poisonous pill, turning everything she touched to shit. The way she saw it, Max should be hooked up with some sweet, prissy little thing he could be proud of, not some overgrown juvenile delinquent who couldn't seem to get her act together.

*Yeah, Ontario—get out of this rotten-ass place and start fresh waiting tables or something. It'll be good to put some distance between us anyway.*

They were in his Jeep and making the three and a half hour trip north to the crossing when it occurred to her to ask, "Aren't you on duty? Won't they wonder why you didn't sign out?"

"I got the desk clerk to cover for me."

"Oh. You gotta work tomorrow?"

"I'm on the late shift. Don't worry about it."

Riley had fallen asleep by the time they got to Picton, buzzing softly through pursed lips, just like when she was ten. They'd reached their destination, but Max let the motor run and stared at her for a few more minutes, just like he used to when he was twelve.

He shut off the engine and the sudden stillness made her eyes blink open.

"Wow, how beautiful." Beneath the darkness, rose mixed with amber over the lake, stretching to eternity from his Jeep and the small cottage nestled among the pine trees at their right.

"We're here," he said.

"Where's here?"

"Home, baby. We're home."

"What the fuck are you talking about?" Riley asked in a mix of terror and delight.

"This is home, Riley, if you want it to be." Max put his hand on her knee, squeezing softly and pressing his lips together, waiting on her reaction.

Riley couldn't help herself; she smiled wide and free for all the things she didn't allow herself to think about—the happiness she was so afraid of, because happiness never lasted.

Her grin was more than he could have asked for, celebrated by his own as he bounced out of the Jeep to fish the house keys from his pocket. He tried to steady his hands on the lock, so excited to show her the home he'd been saving up for since he started with the department.

"Not much to look at now, but wait until I finish painting and change the carpet." He turned to her. "I was gonna get it all fixed up before I showed it to you, but as usual you weren't exactly cooperative."

"Just open the door already."

The place was small, barely a one bedroom, with a kitchenette off a box of a living room that took up most of the entire first floor.

"There's a small basement, where I'll keep my weights. And up these stairs...go look." Max flipped on the lights.

She wrinkled her nose in playful suspicion and jogged up the narrow wood steps. In the attic, a big double window facing the lake poured the new day into the room. In front of the window sat her old wooden easel and a stool.

Riley walked over to it, running a finger over the layers of dried paint. "I thought I told you to get rid of this thing."

"Ms. Perry had it out on the road, but I knew you'd want it back one day. Even when you gave me that crazy bullshit about how you were done with painting, I knew eventually you'd change your mind."

"This easel is the only thing I ever won in my life."

"High school art competition, first prize."

"Countywide," she added throwing a hand on her hip, and then she took a breath, ready to face a bit of truth. "I turned my back on all the things that made me happy, 'cause it was easier to be miserable."

"Bad habit."

"Yeah."

"You gonna finally let me help you with that?"

Riley cocked her head to the side and floated her gaze over him thoughtfully. Letting Max love her was the scariest thing she'd ever do, but the burning in her chest gave her a reason to be brave. Another deep breath and then she licked her lips and stretched her long slender frame. Smiling, she tossed him another question instead of an answer. "You got a shower?"

He shook his head at her chronic evasiveness. "Downstairs."

With a goofy little twirl, she started for the stairs. "You

coming?" Her voice was heavy and low.

Max followed close behind, lifting the hem of her T-shirt as she raised her arms and descended out of it. At the bottom of the steps, she tugged down her leggings and stepped out of them, leaving her Havaianas tangled among the fabric.

When she was nude, Max couldn't keep his hands off her. He scooped her against his angular frame, his anxious hands cupping her breasts and his cock pressing against her ass through his jeans.

"Shower...I need to get clean," she said softly and Max understood, slipping around her and taking her hand.

He led her to the one of two open doors off the living room where a tiny little bathroom had been scrubbed diligently ahead of her arrival. Riley also noticed the neatly made bed in the room next to it.

The water screamed through the pipes, but heated quickly, and Riley stepped in. Max grabbed a washcloth and soaped it, not caring how the water splashed and spilled onto his clothes from her body. He started with her face, tenderly guiding the cloth over her closed eyes and removing the black stains of her mascara. She let the water rinse the soap away and squinted through the droplets caught on her lashes. Max smiled and swept the last of her lipstick away, forgetting momentarily anything else but kissing her, just softly, sinking onto her full lips. Then he resumed washing the past twenty-four hours from her flawless skin, while Riley watched the water spiral down the drain and willed her self-inflicted bad luck away with it.

The cloth was gentle against her skin. Max carefully circled her supple breasts and watched her nipples peak in response. He wanted her to feel his patience, to know his commitment. These were his gifts to her, and he hoped she was finally ready to accept them.

Another kiss for each pert little bud before he continued had Riley pressing her hands against the simple white tiles, needing support. His mouth played happily with her in the warm water as it soaked him entirely. He kissed her stomach and ran the cloth down her tawny leg, over her calf and rounding to the inside of her ankle before making a lazy trail back up to her inner thigh. She widened her stance, and the same attention was given to her other leg without hurry.

Riley loved every minute of her cleansing, feeling more open and free from her emotional prison with every sudsy caress. When Max massaged the cloth into her folds, she eased back against the wall and moaned in time to each slow pass. He looked up at her, to be sure, and his fingers found their place inside with his tongue getting its first taste of her cunt. The cloth was forgotten, clogging the drain.

He knew her better than anyone and despite her tough exterior, what Riley needed was to be cherished—the way he had since the day Social Services brought her to Ms. Perry's porch with her skinny arms folded and her hair in two long braids, looking as lost and angry as he was. For once, Riley eased into the feeling and let it wrap around her.

Just like his tongue wrapped around her clit.

Making her pant like it was a switch hardwired to her heartbeat, he spoiled that sensitive nub of flesh and nerves from every angle, never letting his fingers forget the rhythm he was working inside her. Her mouth hung open, catching water spray as it bounced off her neck and shoulders. Hips swaying to his languid tempo of licks and passes, Riley's hand made it to the top of his head for greater stability. When her knees started to quake, he sucked harder on her clit and doubled his efforts with his fingers until she burst onto his hand, her silk unmistakable in the water. Max stood up and turned off the shower, his other hand extended in invitation to step onto the small, white terry-cloth rug.

His drenched cotton shirt clung like a transparent sheath on his trained physique. He tore at his buttons, treating a shivering Riley to each revelation of his muscled torso. She'd passed countless rebounds to that chiseled milky chest from the edge of their driveway and felt the same familiar stirring in her depths at the mere sight. Then his pants were also discarded and he graced her with a full view of his swollen cock, so perfectly directed at what he needed.

*Who* he needed.

He yanked the towel off the door and cocooned her with it in the same fluid motion that cradled her into his arms.

Riley summoned his mouth to hers, wild and demanding, wanting to crawl inside of him and equally desperate for his entry of her.

"Love me," she managed to whisper as he placed her on the new down comforter. She poured onto it like honey in a sea of cream and Max hovered on top of her, pressing his arms into the mattress while his heavy cock wandered inside her moist nest of neatly trimmed curls.

He pulled away to reach into the nightstand and Riley tried to keep her hands on him, cursing the separation of their skin. With a condom in place, he rolled into her in a series of long churning strokes, pulling a raspy sigh from her throat. Riley usually hated to be on her back, to be submissive, to be taken, but Max was rigid with desire for her and she only felt like a fool for denying him for so long—and denying herself. His eyes were open, steel blue staring into her soft brown, and he meant every inch to delight her more than the last. She opened wide for him, wanting to split herself in two if she could, offering up her deepest recesses.

But Max was plenty deep already, taking all she gave of her body and sucking the rest of her heart from her tongue. She was fire to him, a molten and searing heat that was simply addictive. He could make love to her forever and pour his soul into her for the rest of his life. When Riley wrapped her legs around his waist, bucking and crying out beneath him, he had no choice but to release the seed he'd wanted to give her for so long. And each of them wished there needn't be a barrier between them, imagining a day when there wouldn't be.

"You never gave up on me," she said, her voice cracking under the emotional overload.

Max shook his head and landed a sweet kiss onto her lips.

"You could have, so many times you could have."

"Shhh. That was then." His furrowed brow told her he wouldn't have any more of that kind of talk. "I'm starving, aren't you?"

She nodded.

"There's a diner in town that makes decent pancakes." He paused. "Right next to the police station."

Riley waited intently for him to go on, sensing there was more.

"My mother didn't do shit for me except give birth, and the dual citizenship that came with it."

"So, all of a sudden you're a Canadian, eh?" Riley joked, and propped up onto her elbows.

"Go figure." When Max smiled, his cheeks rippled in a series of dimples that always made her heart skip. He continued, "Last spring I applied with the Provincial Police and they start training next month." Max slid his hand onto hers and mingled their fingers. "This is it, baby. This is our chance to tell the past to fuck off."

She couldn't make any promises. She had no experience in

that area, but she could speak her heart. "I love you, Max." Riley breathed the words, with her chest releasing the weight of her honesty into the air around them. She was positive about where she belonged, with the man who loved her at her worst and made her want to get to know herself again. It was the closest to perfect she had ever felt in her life...and something she could really get used to.

# FORGOTTEN
# BODIES

## Giselle Renarde

S o many encounters seemed to begin this way, with Susan anticipating his desire and slipping into the bathroom. She'd have to bite the bullet eventually, she knew, but claiming, "I have to pee," would at least buy her some time. Sex shouldn't be so complicated. It never was before. What had changed since they married? Nothing. She hadn't changed, Anthony hadn't changed…so why was everything different now?

*Age.*

Goddamn it, what a total cop-out of an answer that was, if undeniably true. Susan faced herself in the bathroom mirror. Even bathed in the soft light of those wall-mounted sconces, her skin looked faded. Naked, her body was a sagging, withering shell of its former self. She hated the way her nipples drooped like they would plummet straight down to earth if they weren't attached to her chest. They'd never be perky again, not without a boob job, and fat chance of that happening. She wasn't the type to have work done.

Susan fingered the bowl of potpourri on the counter, cursing the thick layer of dust coating those faded rose petals. Dead things. What could better complement the harvest gold fixtures and outdated furniture? Everything in this house was past its prime. Last week, she'd found a can of soup that expired in 1991. When did she grow old enough to have twenty-year-old soup in the pantry, let alone a twenty-year-old child in college? And Kyle was the *youngest* of them. Jesus...where had she been all those years?

Leaning over the sink, she met herself straight on, eye to eye. She was her own most fearsome competitor, and she would not be defeated by unfounded anxieties. What was she so afraid of, anyway? Her looks really weren't the big concern, if she was honest. She'd always had lovely eyes, huge as a dairy cow's, with thick curling lashes. Her cheeks were thin without appearing sallow, and her lips bee-stung, plump and deep pink even without lipstick. She would always have a pretty face. The thought made her smile, briefly.

If she was brutally honest, she knew damn well what she feared: that she'd lost her libido and it would never come back again.

It was such an all-at-once occurrence. Her sex drive didn't drain from her body over weeks and months, like honey slowly dripping from an overturned jar. It was there, and then—poof! Gone. Her body had betrayed her in the worst way possible. It had forgotten how to love.

The worst of it was that she remembered what it was like to be young. God, did the juices ever flow back then! All she had to do was glance at the bulge in any random guy's jeans and her whole body would flush. She'd spent her late teens and early twenties perpetually red in the face. Her little brother called her Tomato until Dad told him to knock it off.

The very thought of sex, the passing whisper of its possibility, made her weak in the knees when she was younger. And *wet*. Oh, god, did she get wet back then. Wet was her constant state of being. In college, every professor was "the handsome professor"—even the ugly ones—and she'd sit in those lecture halls daydreaming about what it would be like to kiss them, fuck them, suck their cocks. She had a dirty mind back then, and her actions were almost as bad.

Before she met Anthony, Susan screwed everything in pants. She did. And when she wasn't drinking and smoking and nailing guys at parties, she was teasing her clit beneath the covers or in the shower or on the can between classes. Her pussy was always so hot and ready, dripping with the nectar of her arousal, that she couldn't help herself. It was a compulsion.

Those were the halcyon days of female sexuality. She'd felt so empowered back then, and no less so when Anthony came along. He wasn't just drop-dead gorgeous, but also so supportive of her goals. And, in fact, he was probably even more attractive now than he was back then. Men were lucky that way: like fine wine, they improved with age. Women were more like fruit: they withered in the bowl if you didn't sink your teeth in fast enough. Sure, Susan had had plenty of teeth in her, so to speak, but she just couldn't come to terms with her dry core. No juice left in her. Still, if she didn't pretend, wouldn't Anthony go looking for it elsewhere? And he was so darn handsome he was sure to find it.

She'd been stalling too long now. Anthony would wonder what was wrong, and she didn't want him to know. Actually, she didn't want him thinking anything was wrong at all, because then he'd just try to fix the problem and that would make matters worse. These things always sorted themselves out in time.

Unless they didn't.

With a woeful sigh, Susan rested her shoulder against the door and turned the knob. It swung open faster than she'd anticipated, and she fell into the bedroom, nearly tumbling into the armoire but recovering her footing just in time. She felt like a fool until she realized Anthony wasn't in here. Where had he gone? She'd thought he'd be waiting in bed with that expectant come-hither glint in his eyes.

"Guess not," she said out loud, wandering naked into the hallway. "Anthony? Where'd you go?"

The house was eerily quiet. Usually, they had the radio on and at least one TV blaring. Now all she could hear was the hum of the fridge downstairs. With all this silence, it felt like nobody was home...not even her. A looming absence took hold, and she gripped the dated iron banister, looking over the railing to see if Anthony was down there. She couldn't recall the last time she'd been naked out here in the hallway. Probably never. There was something strange, she thought, about those households where family members walked around naked. It seemed far too intimate for her liking.

*Slap!*

Something hit her ass—hard—and she whipped around to find Anthony standing between herself and the bedroom. She still hadn't put together what had smacked her, or why, but at first the event alongside her husband's appearance seemed purely coincidental. He wouldn't have hit her. He'd never done anything like that. Maybe the roof was caving in and a piece of the ceiling had fallen on her behind. She looked up, but nothing appeared out of the ordinary, and there was no debris on the carpet.

Susan turned her attention again to Anthony, who was fully undressed now, his cock already hard in anticipation. The sight of his erection made her stomach clench, and she welcomed this new mystery as a preventative distraction. "Did something just hit me in the ass?" she asked.

"Yes," he replied, drawing out the *s* sound.

He was grinning at her. His hands rested against his hips like he had no shame. That Cheshire smile grew, and finally he tossed his head back and laughed.

"What?" She didn't understand what was going on, but it was beginning to dawn on her what had happened. "Did you just spank me?"

When he raised his hands from his hips, she flinched, but it was only to clap them together in front of his chest. "Yes, I did." His eyes shone bright with an unfamiliar brand of lust. "Did you like it?"

What a question! *Did you like it?* "Well, I didn't expect it." Now she recognized his game, but quickly realized she didn't know how to play. "It was certainly a surprise."

She kept an eye on him as he approached, but tried not to appear as dubious as she felt. If this was what he wanted, this was what she'd give him. Ultimately, what difference did it make? She no longer took pleasure in anything that used to turn her on. He could put on a pair of stiletto boots and throw spaghetti at her if he got off on it—anything to keep him at home.

"Did you..." She stammered, tripping over her words like untied shoelaces. "Do you want to do it again?"

He cocked his head, smirking. "Oh, yes."

Wonderstruck, she turned around, gripping the slick iron railing. Where was this coming from? What was the appeal? He spanked her again, without any real warning, and she jerked forward against the banister. It didn't hurt, not exactly, but she definitely felt the smack. Once his hand was gone, her flesh felt a tad warm. She looked back at him, shocked, but he was already gearing up for another blow.

On reflex, Susan squeezed her asscheeks together to quell the sting, and it worked to a degree, but she found she'd preferred the sensation when her muscles were lax. Leaning down across the railing, she let her breasts hang over the side and marveled at the distance between herself and the first floor. All she could do was hope the banister would sustain her weight.

Anthony spanked her again while she was distracted by heights and dangling breasts, and she felt that one like the crack of a whip. It burned where he struck her, and the warmth spread throughout her body as another smack rained down on her ass. He alternated between one cheek and the other, but his spankings were so effortful and sharp that even the rotation provided little relief. Her ass burned. Even when he rubbed her cheeks in a figure-eight motion, she could feel the smolder beneath his palm.

The worst part was not knowing when the next one would come. She wriggled against his hand, but he held her with the other, now scooping his entire forearm around her belly to keep her in place. He obviously didn't want her scampering away and obviously knew she had it in mind to do so. It wasn't fear. No, it was a queer brand of anticipation, an exciting sort of dread, even. Her heart raced. She felt like a hunted animal, though she was already caught in his trap. Her body rubbed against him when she felt his hard cock digging into her side, but that was just a pleasant distraction before the next one came.

He spanked her three times in succession—one, two, three— all in the same spot, and it hurt so goddamn much she cried out against the pain. Yes, it was agonizing, really and truly, but when she writhed against his firm grip, she hoped he would keep her in place. She didn't want to be hurt, but she also did want it. Did it feel good? No. It was horrible. It hurt like hell.

But when he slapped her again, the other cheek this time, hot and fast, did she like it? Yes.

She felt his hand coming down on her, and she just couldn't bear any more. Reaching back, she shielded her ass with one hand, but he grabbed her wrist and set her palm back down against the railing. He spanked her before she could block him, and she screamed his name, more an ejaculation of surprise than of pleasure.

"You want me to stop?" he asked, spanking her again.

Susan bit her lip, grasping the iron holding her up. She couldn't bring herself to say yes, or even to say no. When he smacked her ass, it burned. It burned like hell, but she wanted him to take her right to the edge and then hurl her over.

"Should I stop?" he asked again.

Her voice was small, rising from some hidden place inside of herself: "No."

Even so, when he smacked her once more, she reached out to block him. He managed to avoid hitting her arm, but grabbed her wrists and forced them around her front until her hands cupped her swinging breasts. "Keep those fingers busy," he said, smacking her without warning.

It hurt. Oh, it hurt, but she pinched her own nipples as he waled on her ass, and sparks of electrical pleasure ran from her tits to her clit. Her circuitry was frying like an explosive power box, and the pain of his spanking combined with the delicious ache in her nipples as she pressed them between her fingernails. That hurt, too, but she didn't stop the torture. She hung over the railing, looking down at the carpet in need of a pass with the vacuum, the little table strewn with unopened mail, the laundry basket en route to the basement, and she closed her eyes to all things mundane.

She pinched her tits. Anthony smacked her ass. Pleasure-pain swirled in her belly, and she heard herself crying out against the swollen, blazing flesh of her ass and the self-imposed sting of her nipples as she teased them. She didn't know what she was saying, and she didn't think they'd gone too far until she felt something trickling down her thigh. Oh, god, she was bleeding.

"Stop," she said, reining reality back in. "Anthony, stop it now. Stop it!"

He did, stepping away from her. When she turned to look at him, he was smiling even wider than before. His expression fell when his gaze met hers. "Honey, what's wrong?"

"I'm bleeding," she said. Wasn't it obvious?

"Where?"

Susan strained, trying to get a good look at the back of her thigh. It was no use. Her glowing red ass was blocking the way. "From my..." She wasn't exactly sure of the answer.

Reaching down between her legs, Susan found her pussy lips engorged and slick with something. She lifted her fingers to the level of her eyes, and the late afternoon sun streaming through the skylight caught the gleam of a clear liquid. She knew what it was, of course, but she didn't dare believe it. It was *her*. It was *from her*. She'd become so turned on with the spankings, her juice wasn't just flowing but gushing, even dripping down her thigh in a healthy stream of liquid arousal. This couldn't be for real. It was so much like a wonderful dream that she feared waking up.

A growl rose through Susan's throat as she turned to her grinning husband and pressed him into the bedroom, closing the door behind them as if some voyeur might see what would come next. She still couldn't really believe it, but the evidence was right there between her legs. Her body remembered what it had forgotten, and now it was going to show him a thing or two. Now she was raring to go.

# IN THE DOGHOUSE

## Hanna Martine

C onfetti rained down. The director yelled, "Cut." Interns
quickly ushered the studio audience kids from the soundstage so they wouldn't witness the inevitable smackdown
between Petunia the Puppy and her lovable friend Jim.

Brad didn't want to witness it either, and he *was* Jim.

Mary ripped off Petunia's huge costume head and charged.
Her graying hair was damp, her face red and swollen. "Could
you be a bigger ass?"

Thank god her role on the show was silent. Brad snapped
off his polka-dotted suspenders and drew a deep breath before
answering, as calmly as possible, "Let's try to be professional
here. I'm sorry…"

"Professional?" she shrieked. "You tripped me. The kids
couldn't stop laughing. You delayed production."

Everything was always about her. *She* was the show-biz
veteran. There was a Petunia the Puppy long before she found
a suspendered friend named Jim, and she never let him forget

it. The show hadn't earned national attention until he'd been brought on, but he'd never remind her of that.

"It was an *accident*, Mary."

"Yeah, right." She stomped off. All five feet of her.

The truth was, as his contract wound down, so did his enthusiasm. He'd gotten sloppy. He knew it. So did Colson, the producer.

Brad whirled, kicking aside balloons and confetti. As he shoved his way backstage, his arm snagged the corner of Petunia's doghouse. The rough plywood drew blood and he hissed, willing himself not to scream at the rafters in frustration.

In his dressing room, he collapsed into the black vinyl chair and stared up at the ceiling. The crack there had lengthened since last week.

A production assistant popped his head in. "Colson wants to see you."

On the dressing table, Brad's phone buzzed to life. *See me*, flashed Colson's text.

Then, over the soundstage intercom: "Brad and Mary to the producer's office. ASAP."

Nothing like a little overkill to remind him he wasn't the star when the cameras were off.

Adam, this spring's intern, entered and slapped clipped pages on the counter. "Script change for tomorrow."

Brad sighed. "Of course there is."

"Hey, we still heading out tonight?"

"Sure. Meet you there at nine."

Adam left, looking all giddy to be hitting a club with a "television star," and Brad kicked the door shut.

A new set of accusing eyes burned into him. "What?" he snapped at the packaged doll on the dressing table. Jim's face—*his* face—in plastic perma-smile, the ever-present suspenders, all personality and genitalia carefully erased. With a hard slap, the box tumbled to the carpet. The back of it mocked him with a picture of Petunia, her felt tongue sticking out at him like a child's.

He wondered what Greg Burkowski, his best high school bud, had thought when he'd first seen the doll. Greg had been the actor wannabe, and Brad had driven Greg down to Chicago for the "Doghouse" audition. Brad had only read for the scouts to support his friend, to prove to Greg he was better than at least one guy there.

After, they'd driven home northwest on I-90 in mostly silence, Brad's callback hanging between them.

Six years ago, he never thought he'd want out. His first acting job as star of his own show? Screaming fans—even if they were barely old enough to use the toilet? Kick-ass apartment overlooking the Hudson? Yes, please.

Now he glared at the small stack of paper shoved partly behind the mirror. Three more years up for his taking. *Fuck.*

The groove he'd fallen into had mangled his soul. He wasn't going to snag any more acting gigs. He was Jim from "In the Doghouse," period. And until recently, his paycheck had made that okay. But he didn't want to end up like the Zookeepers— three fortysomething guys who'd been singing the same damn animal songs for going on twenty years now.

Coward. He didn't have to be an actor. He didn't even have to stay in New York. He could go back to school, reapply to the Miami of Ohio architecture program he'd been accepted to before moving to New York one month before classes began.

But he was so damn comfortable. And so damn weak.

That night he met up with Adam at a club that used to be the hottest thing since hell but had since mothballed its velvet rope. All Adam wanted to talk about was the show and how exciting it was. Brad knocked back a few and let the alcohol do its thing, and soon he wandered off in search of people who hated their jobs as much as he did.

Sweating whiskey glass raised above his head, he weaved through the crowd. A woman deliberately pressed against his side, tits bracketing his elbow. Softness, fullness. How could he not turn?

"You're Jim," she said. "From 'In the Doghouse.'"

No one his age ever recognized him. His show wasn't exactly the thing people in their midtwenties watched while recovering from their hangovers.

Faint lines crossed her forehead and deeper ones radiated out from her eyes when she smiled. A low-cut dress revealed a sun-damaged chest. The press of bodies in the bar didn't allow him a head-to-toe look, but he guessed the dress was probably a bit too short. He knew these women, these moms whose nights on the town called for outfits they'd never wear in their day-to-day life. They liked to have one too many drinks and laugh loudly. They proudly wore their crazy, fun confidence.

And he liked to watch them.

He ran a hand through his hair and he watched her watch it. They usually commented on how different it looked without the slick of gel. Girls his age didn't notice at all. "It's Brad, actually."

"Brad, huh?" She quirked her head to the side, dark-brown hair swaying in shiny layers. "I like it. You're taller than I thought you'd be."

"How about that? Usually people tell me I'm shorter."

She shrugged, a faint line of muscle appearing in her upper arms. "I'm not exactly a giant."

The crowd eased a bit and he snuck a glance at her body. She was a tiny little rocket ship balancing on three-inch heels.

And yeah, her dress was a little too short, but he wasn't complaining.

Her legs looked strong, covered with that layer of softness that age so lovingly slathered on. He was strangely drawn to the place where her knees came together. He imagined sliding his hands between them, pushing them apart.

Usually about now women would whip out their camera phones and click a picture, giggle and then send it back home to their friends. Then they'd leave and he would try to talk up a recent college grad who would laugh uncomfortably when he told them he hosted a show for preschoolers.

"I'm Cara."

She had a firm handshake, one that said she knew how to handle people. She held on longer than necessary, her fingers dragging leisurely through his. He knew what that meant, too. She smiled mischievously out of one side of her mouth, a pale crescent marking her skin at its corner.

"How old are your kids?" No use beating around the bush.

Cara smiled lovingly, but there was strain behind it. "Six and seven now. We used to watch you when you first came on. Every morning during breakfast. Now, not so much."

"You should give us another shot. The storylines are edgier."

She laughed, head thrown back so her hair swished over her shoulders. The sight of it did something to his dick.

It was a sign he should walk away. He never knew what women weren't saying. What they'd left at home that night. A popular kid show host breaking up a marriage? He hated his job, true, but the last thing he wanted was to be splashed across the Internet. Greg Burkowski would probably get a kick out of that.

"It's crowded in here." She crept closer. He carefully retreated.

She looked right in his eyes. "I'm not married. I dumped the asshole after he drove to Vegas on another guys' trip, leaving me in the middle of Bumfuck, Iowa, with a one-year-old and a baby, no money and no car."

He blinked, the last gulp of Glenfiddich going down hard. "Wow. You're really direct."

"And you're really, really cute."

The eye roll came involuntarily. His feet took the cue to walk away.

"Wait. Sorry." Her fingers wrapped gently around his forearm, bare since he'd rolled up his sleeves. The scratch the doghouse had given him earlier stung. The sensation of her hand, chilled from holding her cocktail glass, lasered straight to his crotch. "Bad word?"

"Kinda."

She hissed through her teeth, looking sheepish and very, very hot. "Again, sorry."

What was it about this woman? "So...you live in New York now or...?"

"Visiting a high-school friend and her husband." She gestured to a couple sitting at a table near the door. "First time here. First time anywhere, really. I actually gave myself a few days off. The kids are with a neighbor. And here I am."

"Gave yourself?"

"I manage a small chain of teen clothing stores. Started out behind the register when I was sixteen." She sipped the last of her drink and muttered, "Didn't really have any other choice."

That explained the dress. He didn't mind. Not at all.

"Where's home then?"

"Still Iowa." A curtain fell across her face and it was the color of disappointment and shame.

He gave her a reassuring elbow nudge and leaned closer. Her

faint perfume cut through the beer and vodka smell of the bar. "Yeah, there's a Midwestern look about you."

She wrinkled her nose. "I deserve that for calling you cute."

"Nah. Recognize one of my own. La Crosse, Wisconsin."

"Get out! Really? That's only a two-hour drive from me."

It settled something between them. They talked about home for a bit, her descriptions of isolated towns and slow days lodging a hard rock in his chest.

Around midnight, when the small-town comparisons thinned, she bit her bottom lip, wearing away a small line of burgundy lipstick. "Do you want to take me home?"

*Yes.* "Is...is that what you want?"

One hand rose to her forehead. An exasperated mom. "Just tell me what you want me to do, Brad."

"What?" He sounded like an idiot. A young idiot.

"Look, I know I came up to you. But can I be totally honest? I'd hoped you'd take the reins." When he just blinked, her hand clenched into a fist. "If I have to make one more decision, tell one more stupid employee what to do, correct one more mistake, break up one more kid fight or tie one more goddamn shoe-lace, I'm going to scream." Her voice rose and rose until the end cracked like a whip.

He went utterly still. Did she truly offer what he hoped? What he needed?

He took a chance, slid a firm hand behind her neck and bent close to her ear. "Get your coat."

Her body stiffened, then melted under his fingers. The skin underneath her heavy hair turned hot and pliant. *Anything you say*, it murmured.

As he pulled her to the door, the local friend grabbed Cara's arm. "Where on earth are you going?"

Cara looked at her wordlessly then lowered her eyes to the

sticky floor. She edged ever so slightly toward Brad.

"She'll be fine," he said. "She's with me."

Cara gave him a diamond smile.

They burst out onto the street. Excitement and relief shimmered around her, and he cloaked himself with it.

It had started to rain, the Soho cobblestones glistening with black dots. Cara belted her trench coat, trapping her hair against her neck. The sleek, dark oval around her face made her blue eyes blaze.

"Take your hair out." His voice sounded froggy.

With one hand she freed it, twisting a thick, dark line down the front of the tan coat. He reached out and fingered the ends of her hair. Underneath the brown strands and the trench coat were freckles he'd kill to see again.

The rain fell harder. Big fat drops that sounded like footsteps.

"Close your eyes," he said.

Her eyes turned misty, then she did as he ordered.

"Tilt your head back a bit. Yeah. Now open your mouth."

The rain dripped into her eye shadow, made a silver trail from her nose to her ear. The water splashed her lips. Her tongue flicked out to catch the drops, and he watched the liquid sink into the moist, pink opening. She swallowed, her throat working, then opened her mouth for more.

He lunged for the curb to catch a cab.

They said nothing during the short ride to the Village. He sensed her sneaking sideways glances, awaiting his cue, but he didn't want words. He wasn't sure *what* he wanted to do to her. He was like one of the kids he saw every day, those toddlers who begged their moms to take them to see their favorite show, and then when they got there they were so excited all they did was either run around in circles or stare like a statue.

The options were endless. He couldn't concentrate. All his fantasies played like a movie in fast-forward.

In his dark apartment overlooking the Hudson, he told her to take off her coat. Cara slid it from her shoulders. No shrugging, no tugging. Just a smooth removal.

She breathed quickly. Stared at him with her mouth slightly open. God, he wanted to kiss her. He wanted...suddenly he knew *exactly* what he wanted.

The thought of it made him bone hard. Shamed him a little.

"Put your coat in the guest bedroom. First door on the right."

She turned. Her ass swayed. Her heels clicked on the parquet floor. She had great calves.

He followed, predatory and silent, three steps behind.

She opened the guest bedroom door and gasped, coat dropping to the floor. She whirled back to him, one manicured hand pressed to her grin, eyes incredibly wide. "Is that...?"

"Yeah." He'd allow a departure from their little game. A short one. "From the first season. Network wanted a different style of Petunia's doghouse for the second season so the producers gave the old one to me."

"Wow. Very cool."

Was it? He never came in here. Had deliberately forgotten the existence of the garishly colored, jauntily constructed doghouse until Cara had entered his apartment. Like so much else in his life, he'd pushed it aside.

She faced him and lifted her chin like an obedient little dog waiting for a treat. Game on.

He raised his rain-streaked arms and braced them on either side of the doorway, encasing her. Her perfume stroked him with invisible fingers. Hands still clenching the doorjamb, he bent down and rubbed his cheek against hers. His tongue found her ear, licked around it.

She whimpered. He craved her thighs around his hips.

He'd always fantasized about having sex on set. A twisted scenario he'd never told anyone. At least here no one would catch him.

"Why don't you get in." It wasn't a question.

She froze, then gave a short, choked laugh. "What?"

He pulled back some, unable to stifle the grin. Did she really want to play? "You heard me. Get in the doghouse. I don't want to have to ask you again."

She was so still he worried she might bolt, that he'd asked too much. Or that it was simply too weird. If she called it off here and now, he'd understand. He'd let her go without protest.

Only her eyes moved, dancing left and right. Rain and vodka tinged her breath as she exhaled. "Or what?"

Hot desire enveloped him. Turned off the switch in his brain that warned him to be careful around fans.

He took a half step closer. She took two deeper into the room. There was tension in her stance but her hands looked relaxed, her chin raised. He decided she looked too comfortable.

"Get on your knees."

When she dropped down without pause, his fingers dug holes into the wooden door frame. Her eyes fixed hungrily on his crotch, but that wasn't what he wanted. "Face away from me."

She lifted her gaze, slight disappointment on her mouth, and slowly shimmied around on her knees so she looked into the arch of the green and purple doghouse.

"Now on your hands."

The black dress stretched across her ass as she bent over, showing pinpricks of skin where the weave separated. It rode high up her thighs and he thought for a second she'd stop and tug it down, self-consciousness rising. But she didn't. And he was grateful.

"Crawl."

One knee slowly dragged over the carpet, ass working under the tiny dress. His hands fell from the door, feeling heavy and no longer a part of him. He made some sort of strangled sound in the back of his throat—the sound of a man fighting restraint.

Her head breached the doghouse door and his control snapped. He stalked forward, arm raised, and spanked her so hard his hand stung.

Unexpected pleasure rocketed through his body. His head buzzed with the rush.

She fell to her side, legs in a tangle, one shoulder strap draping close to her elbow. When she lifted her face, her eyes glistened, round and shocked.

Suddenly filled with self-revulsion, he staggered backward until his back struck the wall. Sure, he'd thrown a tantrum or two backstage, but that was because he wasn't that guy who used his fists instead of his brain.

"I've never..." he began.

Oh, shit. She was going to leave. She'd tell one friend, who'd tell two, who'd tell three...and then the whole Internet would know he was a perv.

Cara held up a silent hand and rocked back to her hands and knees, offering herself, back arched so prettily he ached.

"Oh, god." He pulled away from the wall, blood rushing back into his dick.

The look in her eye had said plenty. She knew he was second guessing himself and it disappointed her. But he'd doubted himself his whole life. It was why he'd pushed aside four years of hard, rewarding university work for an easy paycheck and a name on a dressing room door. He'd always taken what was given to him. He'd never stretched for what he truly wanted.

Except now. Cara was giving him something he longed to grasp with both hands.

Control.

He fell to his knees near her head. She looked straight into the doghouse. Her chest heaved, her dangling tits just barely covered.

When he gripped her chin in his hand and forced her eyes to his, there was agreement in her expression. Agreement and anticipation.

"I thought I told you to get inside."

This time as she crawled past him he had a better angle to strike her ass. The jiggle nearly blinded him. The sting vibrated up to his shoulder, even more delicious than last time. She started to cry out then bit it back, a shallow, pleading noise just barely escaping through her nose. Her elbows sagged but she caught herself. Straightened.

She moved steadily inside, the arched opening easily accommodating her since it had been made for a stumpy five-foot woman dressed in a giant puppy costume.

He followed, realizing he'd never actually been inside. Not this one, not the one on set. It smelled of particleboard and dust.

"Stop."

She stopped. The hall light cascaded in through the small windows and painted her body with checkered shadows. She breathed in time with the pulse of his blood.

He moved to kneel in front of her and stared down at the angle of her mouth to his zipper. Her lips dropped open in offering. He felt like denying her, just because she wanted it.

Grabbing her shoulders, he yanked her up so they faced each other, knees digging into the floor. He dragged his thumbnails along her neck and fisted her thick hair. He pulled down hard and laid out her mouth. Took it.

No softness to this kiss. He clung to her hair as though it would save his life. His arms squeezed her little body and she sank into him. She couldn't move, so it was all him. All his own deep, penetrating kisses slanting across her mouth. Demanding her to give him all she had.

When his lips started to smart from the pressure, he pulled back, panting. "You want out?" The flicker of frustration that passed over her face made him feel like a high-schooler again. He didn't like it, didn't want her to make him feel that way again. "Don't answer that."

Instead she slid one thigh between his. "Good," she whispered. "You understand."

One hand released her hair to wrap around her waist. He flung her to the side, pinning her against the doghouse wall. As her head struck the top of the window with a crack, he glanced at her face. Her unspoken message was clear: *Don't you dare apologize.*

So he didn't. He yanked down her dress and freed her tits. He licked one nipple, then the other. A short dart of the tongue, then a graze of teeth. She didn't respond. He bit, the hard nub feeling like candy, at last eliciting a whimper. He did it again. A full-body shudder. The sound of surrender, her own little white flag.

He pulled up on the dress hem, bunching it around her waist. The strings of her thong dug into her hips and formed little mounds of flesh above and below. A woman, not a girl. She met his eyes as his thumbs hooked under the strings. They'd moved pretty fast up until that point, but he suddenly felt the need to slow down. A big reveal, as they said in TV.

Sitting back on his heels, he dragged the thong down her thighs. Her pussy was shaved clean, like a woman who'd known exactly what she was going to get that night. He left the thong tucked around her knees and dragged a slow hand up the inside of one thigh, then the other, watching her shiver.

Then he touched her, sliding between. The thong prevented her from spreading her legs any farther, but he liked that. He liked to dig, to feel the pressure of her smooth, wet folds surrounding his two fingers. And he loved the way her hips thrust to meet him, the way her thigh muscles clenched.

She sagged against him. Her mouth found the crook of his neck and she licked his skin in time to his strokes. His free hand reached behind her. She dripped down her thighs and he followed the sweet path up until his finger pressed inside her. Moans filled the doghouse—his, hers, he didn't know—and he slipped in another finger.

The pressure in his dick bordered on pain. If he took away his hands and stretched her out she'd let him fuck away, but it wasn't what either of them wanted.

He longed for control and she needed release.

Her whole body shuddered when she came. He felt it inside and out, and he could barely hold her upright. Wetness coated his hands. He kept going. Kept pushing inside, kept rubbing circles over her hard clit. Her tongue stopped the movement on his neck only long enough to groan into his skin. For a moment it sounded like crying, but then it was gone.

Reluctantly, he removed his hands and slid them, still sticky, around her waist. Her head lolled on her neck as she looked up at him. Neither one of them was done.

He pushed her to the floor, her dress a twisted belt around her middle. He left it there and pulled the thong off her legs with a snap, leaving her high heels on. She stared up at him expectantly. He undid the top two buttons of his shirt, then grasped it at the back of his neck and flung it over his head.

His belt slithered from its loops. He dangled it like a shiny lure and she watched it sway, a plea in her eyes. "Hands," he ordered.

Without pause, she raised them over her soft belly. He wrapped the belt around her wrists, every tug feeling a bit like his own release, then stretched her bound hands high over her head. She lay diagonally across the doghouse, legs spread, heels framing a corner.

The silence in his apartment roared, punctuated only by the sounds of their breathing. One hand reached down to glide along her pussy again. The other dug in his wallet for the condom he hoped wasn't creased beyond use or crumbling from neglect. If he'd known—like she had—what he'd be doing that night, he would've replaced it. Thank god it seemed fine.

So desperate to get naked, he broke his pants' zipper. Didn't matter. Dropping to one hip, he kicked off his shoes and shoved down his pants. Nerves rattled through him. The sight of her, bound and open for him, made him shaky and uncoordinated. His ankle refused to give up one leg of his pants. He kicked out.

His heel struck the doghouse wall with a splintering crash. A new ray of light seeped in where the wall separated from the corner.

Shit, that felt good. An orgasm of its own.

Three more kicks, each one harder than the last. He shouted with each, not knowing what he said, not caring. Now the apartment filled with noise, with his frustration. A jagged hole yawned and he could see the forgotten pile of outdated clothes lying heaped on the other side.

He swiveled a triumphant gaze back to Cara. She smiled, understanding, and opened her legs wider. As he covered her body, pressing her hard into the plywood, the doghouse gave a lurch and collapsed onto the corner he'd demolished. Under his mouth, he felt Cara jump but he didn't stop kissing her.

When he finally pushed back to stretch the condom down his cock, she whispered, "Fuck me hard."

He paused, eyes narrowed, smile tugging at his lips. "You don't get to tell me what to do."

But that's exactly what he did.

He filled her in one thrust, her pussy so wet he thought he might spear right through her. Then she gripped him with her thighs, with her tight muscles inside, and he pumped and pumped.

He felt like he was sixteen again, all desperation and no finesse. She didn't seem to care, responding with low, husky moans timed to his drives. It lasted just about as long, too. When he felt his cock begin to swell and his balls tighten and his breathing draw shorter, he slid his hands under her pliant ass and lifted it up to pound into her even harder.

The orgasm ripped through him, tunneling into the narrow escape she offered.

He collapsed on top of her. After a few minutes, her bound hands lowered to press the cool metal of his belt buckle into his back.

"Sorry." Now he really felt like a kid, apologies and all. "Want me to get you again?"

She chuckled, and the vibration of it, chest to chest, loosened something tight that had been holding him prisoner for a very, very long time.

"You were perfect." The whisper feathered into his hair. "Just perfect."

When they kissed again, he felt it in his heart. He wondered if the University of Iowa had an architecture program.

Cara gathered her clothes and moved into the living room to dress. She was done with the doghouse...and so was he, in more ways than one.

He lingered bare-chested in the hall just outside the guest bedroom, hands stuffed into the pockets of his wrinkled pants. In the living room, she smoothed down the dress whose polyester didn't remotely betray how he'd abused it. For some reason, he couldn't watch her comb through her hair with her fingers. It was too girly, too ordinary. And she was far from either.

He turned to the destroyed doghouse. He couldn't wait to throw it out, to stuff it in the Dumpster next to a stack of papers that would never get his signature.

"Brad?"

"Hmm?"

She sat on the arm of the couch, trench coat dangling between her knees. She looked like a different person. Her forehead seemed smoother, her shoulders less tense. She was beyond gorgeous.

She looked at him shyly, hair covering one blue eye. "Remember in the second season when you guys did that Irish-themed show and you sang 'Danny Boy' to Petunia?"

Of course he remembered. Singing had always been a hidden talent—too personal to share—until one drunken karaoke night. Word had gotten back to Colson that he had some pipes and the producer had made him sing for the show.

On set Brad had closed his eyes to block out the sight of the white puppy and the open-mouthed kids and the stern-faced grips who couldn't care less. That may have been the last time he was happy at work.

"Will you sing it for me before I go?" she asked.

He took a deep breath, then moved to stand before her. He kissed her once, took her cheek in his hand, closed his eyes and sang. Because she asked him to.

# AUTUMN RAIN

## Michael A. Gonzales

Having just turned eighteen, M. graduated with honors from New York City's renowned Rice High School in May. A month later, his artist mother informed him of her sudden decision to move from Harlem to Baltimore.

"I don't understand," M. whined from across the breakfast table. Behind his uncombed head hung a framed childhood picture of him playing stickball in Mount Morris Park.

"What is there to understand? I got a teaching position at Johns Hopkins and I'm going to take it. Truthfully, I'm tired of Harlem." Of course, M. should have seen this coming; his mom hadn't been the same since his business-suited poppa roared away on a midlife crisis red Harley-Davidson the year before.

"What about me?" Though he was a smart kid, M. had not yet enrolled in college and instead worked for minimum wage as a midtown messenger.

"If you want to stay in New York, I won't stop you. I can't pay the rent, but you can keep the apartment." Truth be told,

M. was fearful of living in the big bad city by himself.

Standing up in her pink fuzzy slippers and coffee-stained robe, she rubbed his head. "You know, the house I'm getting in Baltimore isn't far from Calloway State. Maybe you could take classes there."

Leaving on the noon train the second Wednesday in July (his mother had left a few weeks earlier), M. rode the sleek silver Amtrak alone. Zooming away to that sinister city where a drunken Edgar Allan Poe died in the gutter and which hophead Billie Holiday once called home, M. pressed his handsome face against the cool window and stared at the industrial factories lining the landscape.

In M.'s wandering mind, he pictured Baltimore as a bleak wasteland where dusky kids scrubbed row-house marble stairs on Saturday mornings, beer-bellied men cracked steamed crabs in the basement, a goofy director discovered a shit-eating trans-vestite named Divine, and baseball fans bragged about winning the '83 World Series as though it were yesterday.

"The fact that this dump is actually nicknamed Charm City is the biggest joke," M. joked with his mom in their new house, over a take-out dinner of Lake Trout and French fries, the spicy stench of Old Bay seasoning from the seafood spot a block away wafting through their open window.

It took M. a few weeks to get used to that strange metrop-olis where screeching crows soared across the twilight sky, the ancient architecture conjured cinematic images of film noir back lots and the downtown streets were like a ghost town after eight p.m.

The first week of September, M. registered for classes at Calloway State. Dressed in designer jeans, a stylish shirt and loafers, he sulked into English 101, his first class of the day.

Slouching in the hard plastic chair, he aimlessly glanced around the room.

Contrasting the "boys only" policy of his high school, there were a couple of female cuties scattered around the classroom. "Maybe this won't be so bad after all," M. reasoned, looking around excitedly.

Turning around in his seat while the teacher handed out the syllabus, M. noticed a pretty, cinnamon-skinned punk rock chick sitting in the back of the class. Wearing a black T-shirt and thick glasses, she was nerdy hot. Unlike the usual Calloway State sorority chicks with weaves and perms cascading down their backs, she wore a short-cropped blonde natural that resembled a nappy halo.

Drawn to the seductive light that she was unaware of illuminating, M. studied her curvy thickness, making note of the fleshy breasts beneath the wrinkled T-shirt and the pleasing plumpness of her ass.

Three weeks later, while they were reading Neruda's romantic poetry, the professor assigned the class to write their own verses about love. M. wrote a poem detailing his passion for the bustle of New York City: drunken painters fighting in Greenwich Village, free jazz lofts overlooking a sea of Bowery bums and twenty-dollar hookers hovering around the Deuce. Though most of the other students looked bored as illiterates watching a subtitled movie, the punk chick smiled as he read aloud. Her eyes were seductive and M. pretended that he was reciting only for her.

Slipping into the book-lined sanctuary of the college library after class, M. sat at a rickety table reading the latest *Down Beat* magazine.

Minutes later, feeling a draft, he glanced toward the doorway. With clunky eyeglasses, dark eyeliner smudged over green eyes, and black lipstick, she strolled into the room and sat in one of the wooden chairs at the next table.

Though they had never spoken, he knew her name was Lisa Williams. Wearing faded jeans, a black leather jacket, beat-up black Pro-Keds and a ratty black sweater, she removed the thick Buddy Holly frames. From a dirty knapsack, she pulled out an oversized drawing pad.

Glancing at her clipped red nails and nicotine-stained fingers, M. was distracted by Lisa's nerdy sex appeal. After rereading the same page four times, he finally caught Lisa's eye. Stiffly smiling, he shyly glanced at the shit-colored carpet.

"I liked your poem," she said.

"For real?" Under the table, his right leg shook nervously. "After I read it aloud, I thought it was stupid."

"Not at all," Lisa assured him. Her voice was clear and serious. "Out of all of the others, you were the only one who sounded like you had at least read a poem in your lifetime."

"Yeah? But, I'm really more into photography."

"One thing about your poem, though. I just don't understand, if you *love* New York so much, what are you doing in this ass crack of a city?" Her breath smelt like Juicy Fruit and Marlboros.

"Well, my mom moved here a few months ago, so I didn't have much of a choice."

"Man, you ain't got nothing but choices. Why would you *choose* to live in a city more known for crabs than culture?"

Moving closer, M. noticed Lisa's art pad covered with multi-colored stickers of groups he had never heard of: The Jam, The Buzzcocks, The Damned, Siouxsie and the Banshees, The Clash, Elvis Costello and Madness.

Opening the pad, she said, "Take a look at these. I like to draw pictures with my poems." Drawn in black ink, Lisa's spooky images were decadent reflections of ordinary lives. A stark mixture of melancholy and bliss, the pad was filled with pictures of shadowy streets and cathedral peaks, shattered sidewalks and haunted rooms, nodding junkies and giant rats. Alongside each drawing, Lisa had scribbled surreal poems that made Rimbaud seem like a sober optimist. Her loopy handwriting was more girly than he had expected. "These are so cool," M. gushed as the blaring school bell rang, signaling the beginning of the next session.

"I've been working with writers, artists and photographers, you know, trying to put together a literary magazine," she said. Snatching a black pen out of her bag, Lisa scribbled her name and phone number on a sheet of paper and pushed it across the table. "It's just a bunch of young punks trying to start a revolution."

"What's it called?"

"*Benzedrine.* It's the pill William Burroughs and Kerouac took to bring out their genius." M. nodded, pretending to understand. "We're having a meeting Saturday. If you wanna come by, I'll introduce you."

"I would like that," M said, suppressing the urge to be all "golly gee whiz," in fear that Lisa would realize her mistake in trusting a philistine and revoke the invitation.

"You into punk?" Lisa asked, eyeballing him suspiciously. "Other than me and a couple others, there's not many Blacks on the scene in Baltimore."

"Isn't punk dead? I thought groups like Duran Duran and Culture Club killed that noise."

"God, stop cursing at me," Lisa laughed. "I do hope that's not what you're into, because I can't really be friends with somebody who thinks that Duran Duran is better than the Sex Pistols."

"I was just saying," M. mumbled.

"I'll see you on Saturday."

"I'll be there," he said, and Lisa smiled.

By nightfall on Saturday, a dreary drizzle fell from the ink-stained sky. Above the ancient rooftops, a full moon glowed bright. Splashing through puddles dressed in a light jacket, jeans and his only sneakers, a beat-up pair of Nikes, M. slid on the mushy leaves that swathed the wet sidewalk.

Since the city was in the process of expanding its recently opened subway system, blasting dynamite beneath the streets, it was common to see hefty rats scampering under parked cars or dashing down alleyways littered with broken glass.

M. carried a cheap portfolio case containing his photographs in his right hand and a Canon EOS 650 hung around his neck.

"God, you look like a duck," Lisa laughed, opening the door. "Don't you believe in umbrellas?"

Arty and attractive as ever, Lisa was dressed in red Doc Martens, a red plaid skirt and a tight T-shirt.

"I like walking in the rain," M. mumbled, following her into the vestibule. Handing Lisa the portfolio case, he removed his jacket. "There's something about the fall that inspires me."

"You're one of the Autumn People," she said as they walked through the foyer. "Don't worry, I'm one, too."

Lisa's bedroom was a shrine to everything punk. On the black walls were glossy posters of hard men with various piercings clad in tattered leather jackets. Superimposed over a Brit flag was a picture of Queen Elizabeth's pinched face, a safety pin stabbed through her thin lip.

"It's kind of messed-up, but the meeting was cancelled."

"So, what are we gonna do now?"

"No plans. We can just hang out, maybe go over to the

Marble Bar." Reaching into her pocket, she pulled out a pack of Marlboros and lit up.

"The Marble what?"

Lisa blew a puff of smoke over his head. "It's a punk bar down the block; you'll love it."

"So you say," M. groaned. In the corner of her room, in front of a dusty window, Lisa's drawing table was covered with blotches of ink and a large sheet of poster paper; the drawing was a work-in-progress band poster. The floor was cluttered with worn album covers, countless homemade mix-tapes, *Love & Rockets* comic books and a volume of Guy Peellaert paintings. "Can I get you something to drink?"

"What you got?"

"I think my grandfather might have a bottle of Southern Comfort in the kitchen."

"Where's your grandfather now?"

The murmur of television voices whispered from across the hall. The sickly blue glow of a black-and-white set glimmered under the door. "Poppa James rarely leaves his bedroom, except to go to the bathroom or the kitchen. Since my mother died, I'm the only one around to take care of him."

"Southern Comfort," M. repeated, studying the rough pencil illustration. "That sounds good...Southern Comfort."

"Have a seat," Lisa said, pushing a pile of dirty clothes across the black-sheeted bed.

Returning with two glasses of ice and a full bottle of brown liquor, Lisa caught him looking at her illustration of a giant boom box. "That's for a new group, calls themselves Stereo Situationists." Lisa poured the drinks and they jokingly clicked their glasses together. "Honestly, the band sucks, but doing the poster is good practice. Who knows, I could be the next Jamie Reid or somebody."

"You're always talking about people I never heard of before."

"Jamie Reid was the king of punk art," Lisa huffed, pouring more liquor in her glass. After handing M. the bottle, she pointed to the defaced face of Brit royalty taped to the wall. "Reid worked with The Sex Pistols a lot. That image has been on a bunch of T-shirts and stuff."

"Oh," M replied. "I've seen it, just didn't know the name behind it." Embarrassed, he took a quick gulp of the strong liquor, which tasted like a combination of maple syrup and cough medicine. Immediately a surge of liquid heat swooshed through his body.

Two hours later, the bottle was empty. Tilting the bottle to her full lips, Lisa laughed with the madness of a Godard girl and drunkenly flung herself into M.'s arms. "I've seen you looking at me in class," she whispered. "You like me?"

"Yeah, I like you," he stuttered, wishing he could be James Bond cool instead of a geek with a camera dangling around his neck. Lisa allowed a few beats to pass before she finally kissed him passionately.

Awestruck and nervous, M. relished the taste of her tongue as his damn near virginal dick (he'd only had sex twice when he was in high school) began to swell. M.'s senses spun like a merry-go-round as he slowly rubbed his fingertips down her spine. Pulling back, Lisa swooned breathlessly.

"We can't do this here," she whispered.

"Oh, I'm sorry," M. said, suddenly embarrassed.

Lisa smiled. "No, you didn't do anything, but my grandfather is in the next room." Glancing out the window, she said, "Grab your jacket, I know where we can go."

\* \* \*

Not used to drinking excessively, M. stumbled from the bedroom. Leaving the empty bottle on the bedroom floor next to his camera and case, he thought they were going to the rooftop. Instead, they walked out the front door and onto the rain slick sidewalk.

"Let me show you my favorite part of the city," Lisa slurred, holding M.'s arm to keep from slipping on the wet concrete.

Taking careful, intoxicated steps, Lisa and M. walked four blocks. Stopping before they reached the last corner, she covered his eyes. "It's a few feet away, but I want you to be surprised."

After a few steps more, Lisa quickly removed her small hands from his eyes. Blinking twice, M. couldn't believe he was still in the same working-class town. Looking at the wide cobblestoned street—a gothic cathedral on the far corner, a lovely park with a flowing fountain and phallic symbol monument on the next block—he felt as though he was in a mystical place.

"Where are we?"

"Mount Vernon Square," Lisa said. "Up the block is the Methodist church, and that's the first monument ever built for George Washington."

"And that?"

"That's the Peabody Conservatory," she blurted, pointing to the stately Beaux-Arts building across the street. "It's supposed to be the best music school in the world."

From one of the practice rooms, a nocturnal virtuoso improvised a complex piano solo. With style that weaved various genres (splashes of Schubert, bits of Brubeck, pieces of Preston, grains of Glass), rhythmic patterns and melodic structures, the composition was otherworldly and divine.

Crossing the street, the couple drunkenly descended the stone staircase that led into the tree-lined park. Looking around, M.

noticed that the decorative streetlamps were dim and passing cars could not see inside the park.

Sitting on a wet bench that was between two dripping trees, M. briefly admired the cathedral steeple silhouetted against the moonlit sky. "That would make a great picture," he thought as Lisa stood in front of him and unzipped her worn leather jacket.

When Lisa put her red-booted right foot on the bench, M. resisted the urge to kiss it. Slowly sliding his hand up to her thigh, M. pulled Lisa's plaid dress above her crotch. Though it seemed somewhat anti-punk, Lisa wore red silky underwear and the bulge of her large labia brought a grin to M.'s face.

Pulling the panties down, he shoved them into his pocket. Much to his pleasure, her mound was hairy as a cat's back. Rubbing her thick pussy lips with a steady rhythm, he slowly slid two fingers into her sticky snatch.

"I'd rather be eaten than fingered," Lisa whispered.

"No problem," M. said obediently as she wrapped her arms around his neck and affectionately guided his head toward her musky bush. Adoring the sweet aroma, he felt a tingling sensation run up his arm. As the unseen pianist continued to perform, M. buried his face in Lisa's lap and relished her salty taste as he tenderly sucked her clit.

Quivering, she almost lost her balance. Biting her tongue to keep from screaming, Lisa dug her nails into M.'s neck as he blissfully winced. "God, that felt good," she moaned. Breathing hard, she slid onto the wet bench and quickly unfastened M.'s thick leather belt.

Slowly undoing his zipper, she stuck her right hand into the opening. "No underwear, huh? How naughty."

Pulling out his cock, Lisa held the shaft with her long fingers and gently licked the head. Leaning back against the bench, M.

stared at the cathedral's arched windows and multitiered stee-
ples as Lisa applied her devilish oral skills.

Yet, before M. had a chance to shoot his load, Lisa stood up
suddenly. Almost slipping on the wet, colorful leaves around the
bench, she straddled him and carefully eased his hardness into
her juicy pussy.

While he was grabbing her big butt as she gyrated on his
stiffness, Lisa pulled up her shirt and brushed her breasts
against his face. Picking up speed, the music of their lust and the
swooshing sound of her wet pussy competed with the unknown
piano player across the yard.

"I'm coming," Lisa yelped, contracting the muscles inside
her vagina.

"God, yes," M. hissed, his hot breath warming her nipples as
they climaxed together. Minutes later, still holding each other
tightly as the pianist played the last notes of his strange composition and the autumn rain began again, M. somehow knew
that he and Lisa would be together forever.

# THE LOVE
# WE MAKE

## Kristina Wright

M y boyfriend and I have what some people would call a *volatile* relationship. I call it dysfunctional and addictive. Late at night when I can't sleep and I'm replaying our most recent fight, I call it fucked up.

It's not like Paul and I beat each other. Nothing like that. The only bruises he's ever left on me were during sex. But we fight a lot and we have broken up at least five times in as many years, maybe more if you count the times I've thrown him out of my apartment and told him not to come back. But he always comes back and I always let him. It is what it is, you know? It's just hard to say exactly what it is.

My friends who have overheard some of our fighting or heard about it in the aftermath ask me why I don't just dump his ass and find a nice guy who will treat me right. I could, I guess. But that's so boring. I've dated those guys. The ones who won't raise their voices when they're angry, the ones who will take a few days to "cool off" and then act as if nothing happened. I hated it. Those guys are as boring in bed as they are to fight with. Paul is anything but boring.

What I don't tell my friends, what I don't even tell Paul because he'd say I was the one with the problem, and I don't need to give him ammunition, is that I like the fighting. It gets me hot. Yeah, I guess that is fucked up, isn't it? But I think he likes it as much as I do and wouldn't admit it, either. He pushes me and I push him and we fight. And after we fight, we make up. And the making up is hot and heavy and sweaty and sexy. That's part of the reason I like the fighting, but not entirely. I'm not kidding when I say that fighting with Paul gets me hot. It gets me wet. Soaked. I have to change my panties after one of our knock-down, drag-out fights. I'm just wired that way, I guess. He pushes my buttons to piss me off and that does something to my other button. My clit stands at attention when we're going nine rounds over who was flirting with whom at the bar or whatever. I hear myself saying things I never thought I would ever say to someone I love, with my hands balled into fists at my sides, not sure whether I'd rather slap his face or stroke my clit. Maybe both. Yeah, there's something wrong with me. Right?

I've slapped him a few times, pushing him, taunting him. Waiting to see what he'll do, hoping he'll do what a nice guy would never do. When I started dating, while my friends were being told by their mothers that boys didn't hit girls, my mother was practical and told me not to slap a boy unless I was prepared to be slapped back. The threat of being hit scared me when I was thirteen but it turns me on at thirty-three.

I guess I could just ask Paul to slap me. But that seems a little twisted, I guess. Nice girls don't ask to be hit and I'm a nice girl. Except with Paul. He brings out the bitch in me. With everyone else, I'm this super-controlled, calm, rational, together woman, the female counterpart to the guys I've dated who keep their voices modulated and never swear during an argument. People who know me wouldn't recognize me when I'm fighting with Paul. The problem is, I think I'm my truest and most honest self with him—when I'm longing for him to call me a slut and slap my face. Why else would I stay with him and fight with him? He brings out the worst in me—and I love him for it.

"You're a bitch, you know that?" he asked me once during a particularly gruesome battle. I don't even remember what we were fighting about—I only remember the fight itself.

Paul is a high school English teacher, so he's always careful with language. He'll say I'm *being* bitchy or I'm *acting* like a bitch, but that was the first time he'd called me a bitch. My head snapped back like he really had hit me. Hot tears pricked my eyes, but I blinked them back. I didn't want him to think he'd gotten to me. If he thought he'd gotten to me, he would stop. And I wanted more. A lot more. So I just smiled. That's something else my mother taught me. No matter what horrible insult someone hurls at you—smile. It makes them crazy.

"Only to you, baby," I purred. "Only to you."

The veiled meaning was that there was some other guy who I treated better. Jealousy twisted Paul's face into something ugly, but that primal female part of me that loved the fighting and wanted more thought it was hot as hell. He looked like a brute—and I wanted him to unleash that brutishness on me.

"What are you saying?" His voice was quiet, sinister.

I took a step forward, tears long gone, and smiled sweetly. "I know how to treat a real man."

Lightning fast, he was on me, one hand grabbing my arm to push me up against the wall, the other hand coming up in an arc. I thought he was going to slap me. I really did. Even though I wanted it, was ready for it, I flinched a little.

He blinked, as if touching me had shocked him, and let me

go so abruptly, I nearly fell. Damn. It was my own fault.

"Go on, do it," I taunted him, though my voice had lost some of its previous heat. "You were going to hit me, you know you were. Go ahead and do it!"

I was screaming the words, like a child throwing a tantrum because she hadn't gotten what she wanted. It sounded like a plea rather than a taunt. Paul just stared at me, as if seeing me for the first time.

"You thought I was going to hit you," he said, something different in his voice. "I was going to hit you. Swear to god, I was."

It finally dawned on me why he sounded different. He sounded sad. I took a step toward him, tried to touch him. "Just do it," I begged. "Do it. You want to."

He shook his head. "I'd never hit a woman. I'd never, ever hit you, Jules."

I said what had been hanging in the air between us, the truth that I couldn't hide from any longer, the reality that maybe was starting to dawn on him. "But I wanted you to."

He rocked back on his heels as if I'd punched him in the stomach. "What the hell is wrong with you? Seriously, Jules, who says that? Who wants that?"

My first reaction was shame and embarrassment. I was messed up, something was wrong with me. He'd just said it. My shame was followed by white-hot anger. I said the other truth that was between us, the truth I'd always suspected and was now willing to put into words. "You want to. I know you do. It's why we're still together. It's why you fight with me and push me and let me push you. You want to take it farther—you want to, but you can't."

His hand came up to my face, but too slow to actually be a blow. Instead, he tucked a lock of my dark brown hair behind my ear and gave me another sad, puppy-dog smile. "Maybe. But I can't do that. I'm done, Jules."

I thought he meant done fighting, but he fished his keys out of his pocket and took my apartment key off his ring. Laying it on the table by the front door, he walked out. The door closed with a finality that echoed inside me. I didn't start crying for another thirty minutes, but once I started, I couldn't stop. Sometime later, it started to rain.

At two a.m., after tossing and turning for hours, I finally got up, threw a raincoat over my short gown and headed out into the night. I had only intended to go for a drive, but I found myself driving to Paul's townhouse and parking on the street. I sat there, windshield wipers dashing away the heavy rain, staring up at his darkened windows and wondering if this was wise. I'd already gone this far, I decided, might as well see it to its bitter conclusion.

He'd given me his key back, but he hadn't asked for mine. I let myself in the front door, shushed his friendly lab Charlie, and made for the stairs. Paul's voice caught me up short.

"I'm in here," he said, calling to me from the living room just off the front entrance. "Figured you might show up."

The room was dark, so it took my eyes a moment to adjust and see that he was lying on the couch, one arm tucked behind his head. He didn't seem like he'd just woken up, nor did he seem surprised to see me. I took a hesitant step toward him, not at all sure how to read his body language or his neutral tone.

"Paul, I—" I stopped, not even sure what to say. "I'm sorry," I finally said, though I wasn't sure what I was apologizing for. "I don't know what's wrong with me."

"You want me to hit you."

It sounded like a question, but I wasn't sure how to respond.

Did I? Maybe. Yes. In the right context. How could I explain it to him when I didn't understand it myself?

"Not hit," I whispered, my throat raw from screaming and sobbing. "Not like that."

"Like how, then?" He sat up and clicked the switch on the lamp beside the couch. A warm glow illuminated his face. He looked exhausted, a five o'clock shadow on his high cheekbones, his black hair tousled like he'd been running his fingers through it in frustration.

I raised my hands in a shrug. "I don't know. A slap, I guess."

"Like a spanking?"

"Yeah, sorta." It felt surreal to be talking about this. "But more. More than a spanking, more than my ass."

"Your face?"

I nodded. "Yeah."

"You want me to slap your face when we're fighting—or when we're fucking?"

"Both," I whispered.

"Do you push me to fight so I'll do that, be rough with you?"

I nodded. "Yeah, I think so. I think I do. It's messed up."

He moved to the edge of the couch, resting his arms on his splayed thighs. "Come here."

I went to him without hesitation. I wasn't sure of his mood or what was happening between us, but I trusted him. Despite the fights, the angry words, the years of feeling like we were never connecting, I still trusted him.

When I was standing in front of him, he looked up at me. "You're not messed up," he said softly, pulling me down in front of him until I was kneeling on the carpet between his legs. "I think I wanted the same stuff—well, wanted to do it to you. But that's even more fucked up."

I couldn't help myself, I laughed. He was sitting on the couch, I was on my knees in front of him like I was going to go down on him, but instead we were talking about our mutual desire to do the one thing we couldn't do. "Oh, baby, what the hell have we been doing all this time?"

He shook his head. "Hell if I know. The fighting—it's been off the chain, right? I mean, I never, ever fight with anyone like I fight with you. Never. It's weird."

"Dysfunctional," I agreed.

"And I hate myself when I'm saying those things. Hate you when you're screaming at me. But I can't resist it." He stroked my hair absentmindedly, as if he was petting Charlie. "I try to ignore you when you start pushing me, but I can't resist."

"You crave it," I said, running my hands up and down his thighs to the same rhythm as he was using to stroke my hair. "You need it."

"Yeah," he said starkly, self-loathing in his expression. "What's wrong with me?"

"What's wrong with us?"

We sat there like that for awhile, touching each other as if we couldn't help ourselves—and maybe we couldn't. Maybe this was love, even if it was not what we thought love should be.

He looked at me, searched my face as if searching for some elusive answer. "What now?"

I took a deep breath and let it out in a long, ragged sigh. "It's on the table now. Let's see where it goes."

"You're going to have to take the lead here," he said, pushing my hair behind my ears again as he cupped my face. "This is so outside the realm of my experience I don't know what to do. It feels...wrong."

"But I want it," I said.

He just shook his head.

"But I want it." I was louder, more forceful. "Slap me. Slap my face."

He went still. "No."

I could feel the familiar anger beginning to rise. He was teasing me now, playing with my emotions. "Slap me, Paul. Stop messing with my head. Slap me."

"Why should I?"

"Because I want you to."

He laughed. "Not good enough. Why should I do what you want, when you've been such a bitch to me?"

"And a slut," I said, putting that taboo word on the table, too.

He blinked at me, his breath catching in his throat. "Yeah? A slut?"

"Yeah."

"What else?" he asked.

It was my turn to taunt. "You tell me."

"A little whore," he said, the words sounding foreign on his tongue. "Whore."

I was wet. I could feel the wetness gathering between my thighs, soaking through the cotton crotch of my panties. "You want me to be a whore."

"Yeah, I do. But that doesn't mean I'm going to slap you just because you want me to, you bitch." There was a note of anger in his voice, as if the resentment of the past five years of frustration and miscommunication was bubbling up in him, too.

"Fine," I said. "Slap me because you want to. You've always wanted to. You want to slap the smile right off my face, don't you? You want it so bad you can taste it like you can taste my pussy on your tongue."

His hand cracked across my face before I even had time to blink. It wasn't hard, less sting than shock, but it shut me up.

I gasped, or maybe he did, and we sat there blinking at each other. I instinctively raised my hand to cup my cheek, but he pulled it away and put it on his bulging crotch.

"That's what you want, isn't it?"

I nodded, swallowing hard. "Yes."

"Want me to fuck you, little slut?"

"Oh, god, yeah," I groaned. I pulled off my raincoat, stifling under the weight of it, then stripped my short gown over my head, still kneeling in front of him. "Fuck me."

"I'm not done yet," he said.

This time, I was prepared for the slap across my cheek. Same spot as before, so I really felt it this time. Felt the heat in my face, the throb of the sting corresponding with the throb between my thighs. I stared at him, naked except for my soaking wet panties, thinking I didn't even know who he was. Thinking I loved him, wanted him, needed him.

He grabbed me by my hair and pulled me down to the floor with him. "Little bitch," he growled, dragging me across his lap by my hair and smacking my ass hard with his other hand. "You fucking little bitch, driving me crazy all this time."

I whimpered, my ass burning with every hard slap. "I'm sorry," I said. "I didn't know how to tell you!"

He flipped me over on my back and palmed my pussy through my panties. "Your pussy is so fucking wet. You love this."

"Yes," I gasped. "I do."

"Good," he said, stripping me of my panties with one hand while he got his pants undone and his cock out with the other. "So do I."

He was in me with one quick thrust. I gasped at the onslaught, the sudden sensation of fullness. He sat up, taking me with him, so that he was on his knees and I was wrapped around him as he buried himself inside me. He caught my hair in one hand and pulled it back until my neck arched painfully. Then he slapped me again—not my face this time, my breasts. First one, then the other. I gasped at the sensation, my nipples tingling in pain and pleasure, my clit throbbing, his dick hitting just the right spot.

I came, moaning, whimpering, as he slapped my face, then my breasts, then pinched my nipples hard, once, twice, all the while whispering filthy, nasty things to me. Telling me what a whore I was, what a fucking slut, what a nasty, dirty girl. I agreed to all of it. I even gave him a few more to use, which only made him fuck me harder.

As my orgasm ebbed, he lowered me back to the floor gently—gently, after all he'd said and done to me—and covered my body with his and fucked me. Hard, steady thrusts to get him where he needed to go, to bring him to where I already was. His breath coming in fast pants, his cock swelling inside me, his balls slapping my ass. Paul. Solid, dependable Paul. My boyfriend, my love.

"Fuck your slut, baby," I whispered the words like a love poem again and again. "Fuck your little whore. Fuck me, fuck me, fuck me. Fill my slutty pussy with your come."

He came with a bestial moan, arching up over me, driving into me one last time before putting his full weight on me, our sweat-slick bodies pressed together in a way that was so familiar, and yet so new.

He whispered something in my ear, so soft I couldn't hear him.

"What, baby?"

"I said, I love you," he whispered again. "I love you, I'm in love with you, I've never loved anyone more than I love you. Whatever this is, however fucked up we are, I love you. I want you to know that."

I cradled his head against my shoulder, shifting my hips so

that I could bear his weight for as long as he needed to lie there. "I know, baby. I know it. I really do. And I have never loved you more than I do right now."

As I said the words, I realized how true they were. It didn't matter if anyone else thought we were fucked up. I didn't believe that anymore and I would make sure he didn't believe it, either. He was mine, I was his and whatever "this" was, it was ours and ours alone.

And that was all that mattered.

# IN-FLIGHT ENTERTAINMENT

## Catherine Paulssen

S he exhaled and scowled at the dark skies outside the tiny window. At thirty thousand feet above ground with the sun having gone more than an hour ago, you couldn't tell one cloud from the other.

Patrick's hand brushed her thigh above her knee, just where her skirt ended, and his touch electrified her even through the opaque material of the stockings.

"Hey, everything okay?"

"I'm bored!" Lillie exclaimed. "There's nothing new in *Cosmo*, I've already seen all the movies when we flew to Sydney last week and you are absorbed in your book!"

He chuckled. "You're jealous of Mr. Franzen?"

"I might be."

"Aw." He leaned in. "Anything I can do to entertain you?" She kept her eyes fixed on his lips while he spoke.

"There *is* something." She traced his mouth with two of her fingers.

He kissed her fingertips. "You taste of mango juice."

She covered her smile behind her hand. "I fished them out of the fruit salad."

Patrick nuzzled his lips along her fingers. "And the strawberries, too."

She closed her eyes. "Too bad we don't have a private cabin..."

He pulled back a bit. "Last-minute flight. What can you do?"

"And still four hours to go." Lillie sighed and reached for the magazine again.

"Why don't you try to sleep a bit?"

"I'm not tired."

Patrick watched her flipping listlessly through the pages until one article finally managed to get her attention.

"*How to make him sizzle?*" He laughed. "I'll tell you how to make me sizzle no matter what time of day, every day." Lillie looked up from the glossy page. He held her gaze. "You just show up."

The paper tore as she impatiently turned the pages. "I told you there was nothing interesting in here." She tilted her head. "And that was very sweet of you to say."

He wrapped one arm around her so she could rest her head against his shoulder, then kissed her hair. "*Ten G-spots your lover doesn't know about*," he read the next article's headline out loud.

"Shh." She eyed the other passengers, mere outlines of people slumbering in their plushy sleeper seats or focusing on some in-flight entertainment on flickering screens.

A cheeky glimmer flashed over his face. "Ten? Ha. They settled for too few."

"Aren't we Mr. Swagger today?"

His finger teased the trail from her hairline behind her ear down to her neck. "You know I always hit all ten. And then some."

She pulled a face. "Don't torture me with what I can't have, loverboy."

He grinned. "I bet they tell you about how your breath gets caught in your throat when I trace my fingers along the inside of your thighs." Her body was already giving him its full attention. The nerves underneath her skin reacted to his fingers' every whim. The fine hairs at the nape of her neck rose in the wake of his sweeping touch. She might as well let her mind follow. "But do they know about the effect of using a blush brush instead?" His lips were so close to her ear now that she felt the humidity and warmth of his breath.

"That was...wicked." She glanced at him from beneath lowered lashes. "No man has ever before used something like that between my...my lips."

He slid his thumb under her chin and pressed a kiss to her lips. "I can't wait to hear your voice like it was that night again." The tip of his tongue traced the outline of her philtrum, up to the pointed nose and down again to where her lips bowed into a defiant curve. Her breath against his chin came a little heavier than before. Patrick kissed her upper lip and tucked a strand of hair out of her face. "Or see your body convulse the way it did that night..."

"I have a new brush with me," she teased.

"Then you better sleep now because I won't let you once we're at the hotel."

Lillie placed her hand on his crotch. "I also packed the silk scarf." A playful smile flashed over her face as she felt the short jerk inside his pants.

"Look at you in your preppy clothes, fooling everyone," he challenged her.

"I didn't fool you." She cupped her fingers around the bulge and tapped it lightly when she felt his penis bobbing against her palm. "Besides, this outfit's fashionably retro."

"I see. Are these stockings?"

She crossed her legs, causing the plaid skirt to ride up and reveal the broad top of her hold-ups. Patrick took the hand that was arousing his shaft and led it between her legs. He covered her small hand with his long digits and pressed it against her pussy. Beneath her hand, she could feel her own heated skin, barely covered by the flimsy thong she had chosen to wear this morning, the first traces of wetness dampening the lacy material. His fingertips touched her so lightly, but from the complacent smile that tugged at the corner of his mouth, she could tell he felt her excitement just as clearly as she did.

The magazine fell to the ground.

"Patrick, what if —"

Before she could finish her objection, he moved his fingers—only a little bit, but enough to cause another flash of heat and wetness to shoot between her legs and a soft moan to form in her throat. He brushed over her fingers as he withdrew his hand, moving it down to trace the line where her skin met the smooth black material of her hold-ups.

"Take off your panties," he lured her.

"What?"

"You know you want to." He swept his finger across the thin strip of lace once more, forcing her breath to catch in her throat.

"But..." She sighed. "Not here. We...let's wait until we're at the hotel."

Patrick straightened up, slipped his book into the compartment next to his seat and reached around her for the dimmed lamp. "I haven't even started," he mumbled and pressed the button. "*Reading* about G-spots is only half the fun." He set the footrest of her chair a bit higher and bent down. Lillie smiled as he slipped the black pumps off her feet and started to massage the backside of her right foot.

"Mmm...if we turned the seats into a bed you could sit at the other side and spoil them the way only you can." It took nothing more than a look at his big hands to make her purr at the thought. He circled her ankle and stroked it with his thumb. Rubbing her skin against the bone, he went on to roll her toes between his fingers with a gentle pressure.

"But I couldn't"—he kissed her neck—"be doing this if I were sitting over there."

She bent her head and imagined that they weren't in a plane, that he wasn't still wearing his charcoal chinos and black sweater. Or anything at all. His nose tickled the skin beneath her ears, then his teeth grazed her neck, and she sighed when he softly nipped and sucked at little bits. She turned her upper body toward him and moved her hands up his arms. "And I couldn't kiss you."

He smiled. "So I'm allowed to stay on this side?"

"Let me see..." She opened her mouth and wet her lips. To see his face moving closer to hers was her favorite part about kissing him. Seeing the full, slightly shimmering bottom lip and the perfectly swung upper lip, separated from hers by a matter of mere inches, his breath on her face getting hotter until she couldn't tell which was hers and which was his—she enjoyed it as much as the explosion of feelings when their lips finally touched. He opened his mouth a bit and gently pressed it on hers. His hand held the back of her head as he pulled her closer to deepen the kiss. She closed her eyes when the tips of their tongues touched, and moaned softly into his mouth.

He grabbed her thigh and rubbed it with his flat palm. Lillie slung her leg half around him and felt the chill in her back as the forcefulness of Patrick's kisses pushed her against the window. His hands roamed her body now, crawling underneath her shirt. She felt them, slightly dry and cool on her back, claiming her. Her hands pressed against his temples and attempted to pull him even closer to her—impossible unless she could melt into him by means of some unknown physical marvel.

A whiff made her look up, and from the corner of her eyes, she saw an elderly suit passing by, leering.

"Patrick," she panted. "Patrick, we need to...we need to stop." He willingly pulled back, but the look he gave her made it clear he had no intention of interrupting his game for long. He shifted a bit in his seat and watched her adjust her skirt, resume her upright position and reach for the magazine.

"What are you doing?"

"This is not the place—"

He placed a finger on her lips. "I said I haven't even started."

"But—"

He shook his head slightly. His nose traced her cheek to her ear, and he inhaled the scent of her hair. "I love you," he whispered and placed little kisses on her ear. Carefully, he removed the diamond stud she wore and suckled her earlobe. She bit her lip and beamed at him, then let go of the magazine as his hand crawled underneath her black top. He stroked the soft skin over her spine and amused himself by tickling her a bit, then wrapped his arm around her hip and pulled her closer to him. She gasped when his fingers reached her bra, grazing an erect nipple before enclosing her whole breast. He let them rest there and locked eyes with her, tacitly staving off any protest she'd been about to raise. She could feel her heart beat against his wrist and his quickened pulse hummed on her naked skin.

"I love you, too," she mouthed, and his face crinkled into a smile. He slid his fingers into the cup and around her nipple. They stood up even harder the moment he touched them, and when he squeezed them gently between his forefinger and his thumbs, the sensation shot right to her clit.

She leaned back in her seat and closed her eyes. In the darkness, there was only his hand caressing her and his face inching closer to hers. She was engulfed in the warmth of his body and the tenderness of his lips that kissed her eyelids. Without opening her eyes, she snaked her hand around his waist, tugged at his shirt and softly stroked the small patch of naked skin underneath. "Can't you make everybody else leave somehow?"

His soft laughter reverberated through the silent cabin. "You don't know how much I want you right now," he whispered, then took her hand and uncurled her fingers so that he could gently stroke her palm. Lillie pressed her legs together involuntarily. The signals her clit was sending her—joyous messages about being alive and on fire—were getting stronger, and she considered asking him for a quickie in the plane's bathroom. They *were* flying first class, after all; the bathroom resembled an elegant spa. In the golden lights that shone from the ceilings, she would be able to see his body. Naked.

Lillie sighed. He was breathtakingly handsome in his simple clothes. Without them, he was a sight that made her burn with desire—desire that could be quenched only by the very source that sparked it.

Her fantasy of running her hands along his muscular body was cut short when Patrick's hand crawled up her legs and parted them as much as the tight skirt she was wearing allowed. Now his fingernails skimmed the naked skin above her hold-ups.

"Take off your thong," he urged her. She bit her lip, thrown into a toss and turn between excitement and nervousness.

Sitting up in the velveteen chair, she cast a glance at the passengers across the aisle. No one was paying her and Patrick any attention.

"No one's watching," he said, reading her mind. Fixing her gaze on him, she reached beneath the short skirt and slipped off her thong. Without taking his eyes off of her, he took it, crumpled it in his fist and buried his nose in the gray lace. With a smile, he tucked it into the pocket of his chinos.

Even though the thong had been decorating rather than dressing her, and even though she was still wearing the woolen skirt, Lillie felt exposed. Patrick's eyes glinted at her as if she were naked, presenting herself to him, ripe for the taking. She gulped, knowing there was no use in keeping up her resistance.

His fingers reached the rim of her pussy lips and stroked them up and down in languid movements. He watched her carefully, enjoying every reaction in her amazed, entranced face. Slowly turning her to putty in his hands, he continued to run his fingers along her outer lips, the thrill of it making it hard for her to keep from uttering all the moans building in her throat. He slowed down, lightly touching her damp skin as if absent-mindedly stroking a purring cat.

Lillie spread her legs, hoping it would make him deepen the touch of his finger or expose her clit enough to catch some of his tantalizing caresses. It hungered for a loving touch, a small pittance of attention from his skillful hand. Mischief sparkled in his eyes.

"Want to tell me something?"

She knew she should be annoyed by the smugness in his voice, and for a moment, pride welled inside her. It was soon subdued by the cries of her body to be released from the ever more powerful spell he was casting that threatened to overcome her. Willing to go wherever he wanted to take her, she grabbed his neck and pulled him close. "If we were alone now, I'd be screaming your name."

"And?"

"And? That's not—" She interrupted herself with a small whimper when his thumb tapped her clit. "That's not enough?" she uttered.

"No," he shot back, not missing a beat. She couldn't help but smile. A quick kiss on his lips thanked him for the pleasure his finger was causing her now.

"I'd be screaming your name and begging you to take me. My legs would be wrapped around you, pushing your dick deeper inside me." Her tongue teased him as she kept pulling back, making him move closer to her.

"You'd be feeling my nails in your back while I demanded you thrust harder."

He moved his mouth to her ear. "We'll do all that when we're at the hotel. And more."

"Promise? No working as soon as we get there?"

Patrick kissed her ear, then her temple. "I promise." He placed two outstretched fingers against the heated slit between her lips. "Ride them." She did as she was told and rocked her hips into the plaything. Seeking an outlet for the force that consumed her from within, she held onto his shoulders and squeezed her fingers into his arm.

"Not so soon...not so..." Had she said that? "I mean..." She blushed. "I know we shouldn't but... It feels so good," she confessed.

He slowly withdrew his fingers with a gentle pressure that made her crave their return. Before he pulled them away, he let them dance over her swollen clit. Lillie whimpered feebly. Patrick moved his hand underneath her top and rubbed her hardened nipple with the back of his hand. Throwing a quick glance around, he shielded her body with his, then bent down and bit the visible, erect nipple through her shirt.

"Oh, Patrick..." She stretched her body against his. For several minutes, he made her feel the caress of his hands as they explored the underside of her knee and caressed the nape of her neck, making her squirm and cool down at the same time. Her impatience got the better of her; she knew that had been his intention all along. In an attempt to get more of the delicious treat, she enclosed his hand and led it back up her leg. Instead of giving her what she craved, Patrick drew circles on the inside of her thighs. Circles that slowly approached the entrance of her shivering, moist pussy.

She moaned his name against his neck with more urgency.

"Hand me that, please?" He ignored her request and nodded toward her glass of water. The amused frown vanished from her face when he dipped his fingers into the water and smoothed them over her dry lips. Next, he took one of the ice cubes and threw her a suggestive glance.

"Oh, no." Lillie shook her head and wagged a finger at him.

"Oh, yes."

"No no no no no, sunshine," she objected, knowing it was in vain. He rolled the cube down her neck and licked off the water drops with his pointed tongue.

Bending her head toward him, he kissed her and made her taste the cool feel of his lips. Lillie felt the drops of water trickling down her chest and she anticipated what was to come when he spread her legs a bit farther. Patrick was silencing her with his kisses, so she panted in his mouth when the chill hit her heated clit. She felt it contract at the exposure, then shiver as he soothed it with his finger, the gentle rubbing making the blood rush back and sending prickling waves through her whole body, all the way down to her toes. The next moment, the chill was there again, and Lillie clenched her legs, only increasing the effect of the ice. She hissed, and Patrick used his thumb to stroke her pussy up and down. Desperate for an outlet, she sucked at his neck to keep herself from moaning. Soon enough, Patrick's seduction melted her into a creature that consisted of nothing but trembles and heat. Nipping at his skin with her lips and teeth was no longer enough to release the tension. Lillie wriggled and rocked her body against the touch of his fingers.

With a swift motion, Patrick took his fingers away—just in time for her to notice a flight attendant approaching their seats. She jumped back into an upright position and felt a flush painting her cheeks crimson.

"Is everything okay? Is there anything you need?"

"Thank you, no." Patrick shook his head.

"We're fine," Lillie added hastily. She rubbed her damp hands across her legs and hoped her face didn't reveal just how fine they were.

The Asian woman flashed them a smile and began to walk away. Patrick moved his hand back under Lillie's skirt the moment she had passed their row. He pressed a button on the controller next to his seat and with a soft *swoosh,* a wooden tabletop covered what his fingers were doing to her.

"Excuse me?"

Lillie startled when he turned in his seat.

"Yes, sir?" The flight attendant had returned.

"Could you bring us some fresh water? This is… stale." His expression was polite and cordial, but Lillie could detect the prankster shimmering through.

"Certainly, sir. I'm sorry the quality isn't to your satisfaction. Anything else you might like?"

"Um…" Patrick rubbed his chin. His other hand rubbed a part of Lillie in a way that made her want to kick his shin.

"Maybe—a scotch? With lots of ice, please."

The young woman nodded, and Lillie sighed in relief. She turned her eyes away, using all her telepathic skills to make the air hostess forget her impeccable manners and rush away without asking her for any orders.

"Anything you want, baby?" Patrick looked at her with such genuine interest his performance was worthy of an Academy Award. She flashed her eyes at him and mouthed what she hoped could be deciphered as, *You mean, mean man.*

His finger flicked her clit, and she made a little jumping move that she hid under a cough.

"Ma'am, if you can't decide, I could come back in a minute." The flight attendant had misinterpreted her silence.

"No! Um, I mean..."

"It's my pleasure," she offered.

"Or maybe you think about it and let the nice lady know when she brings my drink," Patrick suggested.

Lillie gaped at him. If he was thinking he could tease her, he was in for a surprise. Her mouth twitched into a smirk. She would turn the tables. At least as much as was possible with his hand between her legs in a maddening grip on her most sensitive area.

"You had this amazing-looking appetizer on your trolley earlier," she said, deadpan, ignoring Patrick's stunned expression. "Something with a creamy dressing. It came with lentil salad."

"You must mean the smoked tangerine chicken."

"Oh, that was chicken? Ah, I don't eat that. Then I'll just have the caviar with blini, please."

"Of course," the black-haired woman nodded with a smile.

"And a small salad. Dressing on the side, please."

"Italian vinaigrette or a mayonnaise topping?"

"Uh…" Patrick pushed one finger into her pussy and crooked it. Lillie gathered all her composure to try to look as unfazed as possible. She knew that if she did this right, she could push him to the edge; in the past, that had always been a thrill. "Do you make the Italian vinaigrette with cold-pressed olive oil?"

"Yes, of course. It's certified organic, imported from Liguria."

"Perfect." She sighed a little and looked at the woman with wide, friendly eyes, expecting her to leave.

"Would you like to try any of our entrées as well?"

Lillie cursed inwardly. She could feel Patrick suppress a chuckle before brushing her clit with his thumb. A twinge of lust zipped through her pussy. It was gone much too soon, leaving her craving for more. All she wanted was for the flight attendant to go as far away as possible, as quickly as possible. But the smirk on her lover's face roused her defiance. She would stand her ground.

"It's a tough decision, I know," said the woman, beaming at her. "We're proud to offer our guests a wide range of delicacies of the very best quality in order to create a dining experience worthy of the finest restaurants," she continued, parroting the company's image brochure. Lillie returned her smile.

"Maybe you could recommend something?"

Patrick rolled his eyes and flicked her clit, adding another quiver to the sensations that were already threatening to over-flow her body.

"If you don't like meat, maybe you would like to try the eggplant Parmesan? It's made with spinach pasta and a very delicious mozzarella sauce. I can also recommend the marinated grouper fillets. They come with an orange sauce."

"That sounds interesting. Darling, what do you think?"

Patrick threw her a *seriously?* look.

She raised a flirtatious eyebrow at him and was delighted when he took the challenge and upped the stakes without a moment's hesitation.

"Whatever pleases you, you know I'll comply." To underline his words, he increased the pressure of his thumb on her damp clit.

"Aw." She hid her arousal in a smitten look and tried to keep her breath steady. "Well, I literally can't decide."

"Why don't you just put your finger"—he twisted his own finger inside her walls, pressing against her most sensitive spot—"on the menu and take whatever it points to?"

Lillie gave him a sweet smile, fully aware that this banter—along with the knowledge that he was in control, no matter how much she bluffed—turned him on. Brushing his bobbing erection underneath the table, she placed her hand on his arm.

"Some things are better if you take your time with them." For reasons too bewildering to consider, their little game excited her more than any hand job ever had. There was a strange pleasure in being his puppet-on-a-string, even though he let her pretend she could fight it.

"Could I see the menu, please?" She looked at the flight attendant with innocent eyes and was handed a glossy light-green card.

While she buried her head in the menu, Patrick pulled out his fingers and took her clit between his forefinger and thumb. Cascading shivers rushed through her body as he squeezed it. Thankful for the cover of the menu, she held it in front of her face and closed her eyes for a moment, savoring the moment of pure bliss.

"Since you like being roasted..." He cleared his throat. "I meant, since you like *food* to be roasted, of course, why don't you take the roasted vegetables with a selection of grilled fish?"

"You could also add that to the grouper. It's a fine combination," the flight attendant offered helpfully.

"I'll have that, please," Lillie nodded, a little out of breath. He had just slid two fingers back inside and was tapping them against her walls. "And, if possible, could you leave out the jalapeño?"

"As you wish."

It was too thrilling to stop.

"For dessert, I'll have the Thousand Delights cake combined with the raspberries from the New York cheesecake, but without the frozen raspberry topping."

"Are you done, *Sally*?" Patrick muttered. The flight attendant flashed him a nervous glance before realizing that he wasn't really upset.

"Oh, sir," she tittered. "It's good when a woman knows what she wants."

He gave her his most winning smile. "You're absolutely right." His stare turned back to Lillie and bathed her with affection. "She's an exquisite person. Everything about her." Again, he crooked his finger. Lillie forced herself to concentrate on the flight attendant, who was repeating the order back to her.

Then again, what did it really matter?

"Will that be all?" the flight attendant asked.

"Yes, thank you." The woman turned to leave.

Patrick's lips brushed her ear. "You naughty—"

"Miss? Sorry, just one more thing," Lillie called after the flight attendant. She cupped Patrick's chin and cooed, only for him to hear. "You started it." He shook his head, laughing.

Lillie smiled pleasantly when the flight attendant returned. "Could I have sliced oranges instead of raspberries?"

"Of course. Would you like them with cream?" Patrick pinched her clit. Lillie suppressed a moan and shuffled nervously in her seat. "Yes, please." As the Asian woman discreetly vanished into the back of the cabin, Patrick turned to her with a dark, impressed look.

"Thousand Delights, huh?"

"You inspired me." She took his free hand, kissed his fingers and gave in to the caresses down below.

When his fingers increased their speed and pressure, she rocked her hips into his hand until the friction became so unbearable she had to suck in air through clenched teeth, the only way to keep herself from groaning out loud.

"Come on, baby, let it out." Her eyes stared at him widely in the bluish light. "Everyone has earplugs in or is sleeping." He smiled at her expectantly and stopped the tender strokes for a moment. She panted.

"But—the flight attendant might be back any minute…and what if someone wakes up?"

Patrick resumed the tease and kissed the skin behind her ear. "Moan for me."

She snaked her fingers around his neck and fondled the small curls that fell onto his nape. "You're amazing," she whispered and let her loving words be followed by a deep moan breathed into his ear. He pushed his fingers farther into her, and Lillie did her best not to scream as she felt her body getting more and more lost in a dark, warm weightlessness. She clenched her fingers around his arm.

Patrick leaned in and searched for her dry lips. He prodded them, enticed her to open them farther for him, and sealed her mouth the moment a silent cry escaped her throat and her hips exploded in wild convulsions completely out of her control. He continued stroking her until the waves ebbed away, then eased her body down in his arms.

"Tired now?" He kissed her hair.

Lillie purred with relish. "Mmm." She snuggled against him. "Would you like to have the grouper?"

He laughed softly. When the flight attendant brought the drinks and appetizers, he canceled the rest of Lillie's order, then decorated a blini with some caviar and held it in front of her mouth. Her eyes half closed, she let him feed her.

"How long did you say from the airport to the hotel?" she asked, stroking his chest with her finger.

"About forty minutes." He took a bite from the small pancake.

"Forty minutes..." She yawned. "I can return your favor twice in the limousine."

# REPUBLICANS
# DON'T LIKE

### Kate Dominic

Republicans don't like blow jobs. The man who considered himself my husband's boss was very specific about that. Senator Danzig swaggered about the den, frowning intensely at me as he downed the last of his bourbon. He was making his first visit to our new Georgetown home, which he referred to as Scott's home. The senator was highly displeased that I wasn't absenting myself for the business part of the evening's discussion, especially since the topic was sex, and he was dealing with a newly elected colleague who was known for not always toeing the party line.

Senator Danzig's stentorian voice boomed as he wagged a pudgy finger in Scott's face. "Beware the sinful nature of this godless city. The marriage act was created solely for procreation. Since Carol is far too attractive, she may lead you into temptation." He paused and eyed me sternly. "Woman, submit to your husband, and if he falls victim to your lustful wiles, at least try to get pregnant each time."

I was stunned. Scott was speechless—so angry even the distinguished gray touching the black curls at his temples seemed tinged red with fury. I could only stare at the half-drunken fool who didn't seem to realize that my tall, handsome husband's daily body-toning workouts kept him in shape for much more than press pictures. Scott had a temper. It took a lot to get him riled, but the pompous ass in the hand-tailored suit had just succeeded.

Fortunately, my husband's driver, Ralph, who doubled as our personal assistant, chose exactly that moment to enter the room and announce that our guest had an urgent phone call from Capitol Hill—on the private line that rang only in the study, four doors down the hall. Ralph had stayed late to help me lift the last of the moving boxes. I could have kissed him for his timing, especially a few minutes later when the illustrious senator stomped back into the library, grumbling that the ill-mannered caller had hung up. By then, Scott had regained his composure and stemmed the tide of profanity that had been the first words out of his mouth. Ralph was quietly unpacking books. And I had a firm grip again on both my own temper and my sense of the absurd. I gave Ralph a quick wink. Then I looked at my watch, announced that dinner was ready to be served, and flounced my apparently far-too-curvaceous, naturally redheaded body down the hall to the dining room.

I'd learned early on that dealing with idiots was an occupational hazard of being a politician's wife. I also knew my husband wasn't one to be swayed by intolerant fools, especially when it came to sex. Scott loved it when I slurped his cock—which I did with great relish, describing what I was doing in explicit, dirty detail every step of the way. After sixteen years of marriage, all I had to do was lick my lips at him—slowly, sensuously, taking my time to suck thoughtfully on my full, lipstick-clad kisser—

and he was hard. Even in public. Especially in public. Which always embarrassed him. Which totally turned me on. Because I never let him wear underwear.

That was the deal. I'd suck him off anytime, anywhere, so long as we were reasonably sure we wouldn't get caught. In return, he kept himself so accessible that all I had to do was carefully slide his zipper down, and his big, beautiful cock would fall out onto my waiting tongue. I'd had him under his desk in the governor's office, backstage at fundraising galas, in the bathrooms at the homes of religious fanatics so conservative they probably wouldn't know what a blow job was unless they heard about it on the news. To this day, I can make Scott blush just by mentioning pancakes. He'd been cooking for a church breakfast appearance. He went into the pantry to get more flour. I followed him—with a finger full of butter. When he saw me smiling, he leaned against the door to hold it closed. I jerked his pants down to his ankles. As his cock slid into my mouth, I slipped my finger all the way up his butt. He shot straight down my throat. He came so hard the door shook.

Of course, our lustful behavior was not something we'd chosen to share with my husband's constituents. Despite Scott's continuous fight for moderate programs and his outspoken defense of civil rights, the bulk of the money that got him elected came from donors who, at least in public, espoused the ultraconservative viewpoints of the extremist religious groups to which they belonged. The fundamentalist ministers really didn't like my husband. But they liked the fact that his good looks, charming personality, and honesty consistently appealed to a wide swath of voters from both parties. As did his down-to-earth policies. The extremists backed him, reluctantly, because they knew he could win—especially with their money—which to their minds gave them the leverage they needed to get him to compromise in their favor.

Scott hated that part, especially in his Senate race. He said it made him feel dirty, like he was selling out each time he stayed silent about a platform issue he disagreed with. However, he was realist enough to know it was the only way he could finance that particular election. He hoped that once he was in a position where he could really influence legislation, he'd be able to push a nonpartisan moderate agenda. And that after he was in office, he'd have enough incumbent momentum to help him raise funds for his re-election when his voting record eventually alienated him from what would by then be his former monetary backers.

However, we hadn't dared alienate anyone before Scott was even elected. To the voting public, we bided our time and continued to be what the media so-often called "the ideal role model of a happily married couple." To be honest, we did fit part of the stereotype. We were happy—always together, usually smiling and enthusiastic. I traveled with my husband, in the background, but knowledgeable and supportive, his friend and confidante. The press knew I was always good for a sound bite when Scott was unavailable. Beyond that, well, we kept our fights to ourselves, we downplayed my background as a time-management consultant and we didn't publicize the fact that when Scott was busy, even his campaign manager came to me for everything other than policy decisions. As usual, Scott's latest election had turned out to be a good move for both our careers.

I also enjoyed the hell out of keeping my husband horny. Over the years, a very few intimate staffers had become aware of our little trysts. Kevin, the PR director, had taken to mentioning when he wanted me to get Scott "extra sharp" for a speech. I think Kevin, evil and efficient political animal that he was, particularly enjoyed that part of his job, especially when we were hot on the campaign trail and his own dates consisted of his hand and a bottle of lotion. He knew I didn't always let my husband come. Sometimes I just polished him for a bit, distracted him just enough to take the edge off tense situations. Scott gave some of his best speeches when he had a hard-on. Kevin was always ready with a smirk and a notebook for Scott to hold in front of himself on the way up to the podium.

Scott's driver, Ralph, was especially discreet. We knew he liked to watch. It had been a bit unnerving the first time I noticed Ralph's reflection in the rearview mirror. Scott had been desperate for relief after a full day of pumped-up speeches and a half dozen unfulfilled quickies in backseats and empty conference rooms.

"Do it, babe," he gasped, pulling my hair back from my face. "I want to watch. My dick feels even bigger when I see it sliding in and out of your mouth."

I licked and kissed and stroked, making each swirl of my tongue as hot as I could while Scott writhed beneath me. I was tickling the inside of his sensitive little cock slit, watching him jump with each poking swipe, when I realized we had an audience. I was surprised to feel myself getting even wetter as I watched Ralph's eyes flick back and forth between the mirror and the road while I teased a bone-jarring orgasm from my husband's balls. The only time Ralph even smiled was when I swallowed the huge mouthful of cum Scott shot into my mouth and licked my lips.

Our quiet arrangement began the next morning. With Scott's blessing, I offered Ralph a permanent position, with excellent pay and full benefits, in return for a binding nondisclosure agreement. Ralph agreed, so long as we guaranteed that his "personal assistant duties" would always include being our chauffeur.

The situation worked out well for everyone. Ralph had a nice house, a secure and comfortable retirement, and I had taken to traveling everywhere with my hand inside my husband's pants. As soon as the door closed on the one-way tinted glass to our mobile bordello, I slipped down my husband's zipper and slid my hand inside his pants. Then I played with him, for however long the ride took, while we planned and strategized, sometimes while I sucked him off. And Ralph watched.

Scott was especially primed after last Tuesday's banquet. We'd been in town six months by then. The stuffy black-tie affair with Senator Danzig had gone two hours longer than planned, and Scott's presentation, honoring the author of a highly effective daycare model for the children of single parents, was almost the last thing on the evening's agenda. His speech had been well received, despite the senior senator's almost continuous glower.

As Ralph pulled away from the curb, I tugged my husband's zipper open and reached into his tuxedo pants.

"Feels nice," he smiled, stretching as he leaned back comfortably in the seat. "I thought that dinner would never end. What a bunch of pompous asses." He shivered contentedly as I stroked my fingers nonchalantly over the smooth, velvety skin of his hardening dick. "Ralph, I need to unwind a bit. Unless Carol objects, why don't you drive us around for a while. Maybe take us out somewhere away from the lights so I can see the stars."

"Sounds good to me," I said, leaning over and kissing the side of Scott's neck. "You pick the spot, Ralph."

"Yes, sir—ma'am!"

Scott and I both grinned at Ralph's enthusiasm as he turned away from the direction of our house and headed back toward the beltway. At least once a month, we tried to give him a full show—something to ensure he kept his interest in his job. By now, Scott and I thoroughly enjoyed this perk of Ralph's employment. The privacy window slid up, Scott turned the mood lights up a bit, and through the supposedly one-way glass, we saw Ralph adjust his extra mirror and flick on the radio—the one Scott and I now knew was really a microphone to the backseat.

"So, Mrs. Senator," Scott smiled, turning toward me and running his hand over my arm. "You're looking especially delectable tonight."

"You think so, Senator?" I chuckled, giving him a quick wink as I wrapped my hand tightly around his dick. "I gather that means you're hungry, in spite of that exceptionally rich dinner we just endured."

"Ravenous." He shivered appreciatively as I rubbed my thumb just below the V of his cockhead. "And I've had enough of those self-righteously 'moral' fools. I don't want to save the world from sex." His eyes twinkled lecherously as I leaned into the touch of his stroking fingers. "In fact, right now, I'm in the mood for something really dirty." With his other hand, he reached up and cupped my face. "I do believe I'm going to bury my face in your juicy, wifely pussy. I just can't decide whether I want to stick my finger up your pussy or your ass when I make you come. Maybe I'll do one after the other, and make you come twice."

"Who am I to argue?" I purred, giving his cock a quick squeeze. "The man who thinks he's your boss did say a good wife is supposed to be subservient to her husband's wishes. I'm ever the obedient wife."

"Fuck Danzig," Scott growled, pulling my hand out of his pants. "He's so full of shit an enema couldn't save him. And the day you 'obey' me is the day I quit politics." I wiggled against him as he kissed me hard. "Now lift that obscenely expensive dress and lean back so I can have my snack. I want to taste pussy." He devoured me in a kiss that left me breathless. Then, as I was still gasping, he firmly pushed me back into the seat. "While you're at it, open the top of that dress. Since you have the most gorgeous tits in the world, I want them out and available when I decide to give them a lick."

Scott's grin made my pussy burn. I love it when he talks dirty. So does Ralph. And while our dear driver loves watching me blow Scott, seeing my pussy being eaten is usually something Ralph can take or leave, so long as he gets to listen. We didn't want him to crack up the car before he found a place to park.

I moved to the other side of the seat, leaned back against the door and hiked up my skirt. I grinned wickedly as Scott's breath caught. I'd worn garters and stockings and a tiny swath of silk panty that would have done a thousand-dollar-an-hour whore proud. The crotch was dark with my pussy juice. The scent of wet pussy filled the back of the car as I spread my legs wide and rested the backs of my spiked heels against the leather upholstery.

"Come and get it, hot stuff." I rubbed my finger over the wet spot between my legs. "Dessert is served."

With a curse, Scott tore off his jacket and threw it on the floor. Then he knelt down, lifted my hips and yanked my pussy up to meet his lips. "I love it when you dress slutty."

I felt the smooth vibration of the car entering the expressway as Scott's mouth rained molten kisses between my legs. His tongue poked against my panties, worming its way under the edge of the silk.

"Do it more." I groaned, burying my hands in his carefully-coifed hair. "I love it when your tongue slides under my panties." I thought I felt the car swerve a bit, but I ignored it. I knew things were heating up enough that Ralph would soon be pulling off into one of his favorite secluded parking places.

Scott tickled the edge of my slit until I was gasping, then moved his tongue back out and kissed the wet silk.

"That's just a taste, babe. If you want more, put your fingers on your tits and prime them for me."

As his tongue stilled, I lifted my hands to my nipples, urgently brushing over the soft flesh. The tips stiffened immediately under my pinching fingers. I knew Scott was stalling. He'd felt the same swerve I had and was waiting until the car stopped to continue. Maybe Ralph wanted to watch tonight, after all. I moaned loudly, circling my palms over the hot points, while Scott rubbed his cheek against my thigh, his fingers stroking the back of my knee. A moment later, the car slid to a stop, and the engine fell silent. In my mind's eye, I pictured Ralph taking out his cock. I sighed in relief as Scott's open-mouthed kisses covered my labia and his tongue snaked under my panties again.

"Somebody's horny," he chuckled. I shivered as the vibration traveled all the way down his tongue. "Somebody's pussy is wet and slippery and salty. I bet if I licked long enough, I could make you scream." Scott's teeth tugged on the sopping panties. "But I can't quite reach what I want. Your cute little clit is hiding under this damned silk." I groaned loudly as he rubbed his face over me. "And I can't get my tongue deep enough in your pussy." I felt his hands at the waistband of my panties. "What am I going to do about that?"

I jerked at the sharp rip as Scott tore my panties off me. He lifted the sopping crotch to his nose and inhaled deeply, smiling. Then he held the shredded scrap to my face. "Tell me what this smells like, babe. Be real specific."

I knew what Scott wanted—how turned on he got when I described in filthy detail the things Ralph couldn't sense through the glass. "My panties smell musky, like hungry pussy." I parted my lips and touched my tongue to the dark center of the wet fabric. "They taste salty and slippery and tangy, like a pussy that really wants to be eaten."

Scott's eyes flared. I knew I'd gotten to him. He reared up over me, pushing my hands out of the way, and sucked my breast into his mouth.

"God, you have beautiful tits."

I yelped as he bit on the tender tip.

"Tell me what you want."

"I want you to suck my nipples until they're sore," I panted, groaning as he slipped the other one into his mouth. The sensation of his deep, thorough sucking flowed from my breasts to my pelvis in waves. "Then I want you to eat my pussy some more."

I gasped as Scott bit again, this time on the other nipple. He moved back and forth, tugging long and hard on each one, until my pussy contracted whenever his lips closed around a well-sucked tip. He was breathing hard when he lifted his head.

"I'm hungry for a pussy snack." He gave my nipples one last lick. I squirmed as he slid back down me, his silk shirt dragging over my exposed skin. "My, my, what have we here?"

I heard the appreciative laugh in Scott's voice. I knew he'd just realized what I'd done—and that he'd give a better play-by-play than I was capable of at the moment. When I didn't answer, he kissed the smooth skin of my labia.

"Somebody's shaved away everything but a pretty little red thatch, right at the top. It looks like your pussy's outlined in flames." I smiled as he tugged at the small patch of carefully trimmed pubic hair. He loved my being a natural redhead. "There's nothing as sensitive as newly naked skin. I bet my tongue would really get to you if I licked all over your nice, smooth pussy."

His tongue felt so good, I thought I was going to pass out. I kissed my pussy lips up against him, whimpering as he kissed me back, his mouth making love to my vulva, over and over again. Finally, his firm, strong hands pushed my thighs as wide open as they could go.

"I want to watch you come, babe. Let me hear how much you love it."

I didn't try to hold back. I arched into his iron grip, letting him hear every wild moan and cry as he dragged his wicked hot tongue over the full length of my slit. He lashed my clit, working the hood over the exquisitely sensitive nerves beneath until the swollen nub grew so engorged it had to poke free. Then he started to suck. Hard.

I ground against him, shrieking. The heat of his mouth closed over me, and all I could do was scream in ecstasy as he pulled a bone-shattering orgasm from me. I shook uncontrollably, crying out in relief as his long, strong fingers slid up into me. The hunger was building again, this time deeper, the ropes of sensation tugging outward from far inside my belly. I looked down to see his face smiling up at me, shiny with my juices and his spit.

"Do it again," I panted, grinding myself against him. "Shove your fingers in me and fuck me senseless. I want to come again, damn it!"

Scott laughed and buried his face between my legs again. "Anything you say, lover."

The pressure was just right, just where I needed it. I yelled as my pussy spasmed again, tugging on my breasts viciously, thirsty again for the sensation rushing deep inside me.

"Ooh, you are greedy tonight." Scott flicked his tongue over my clit, lubing me with his saliva. Our mixed juices ran downward, sliding over my labia and into the crack of my ass.

I was vaguely aware of him tearing his clothes off. Then he

yanked me all the way down onto the seat. The next thing I knew, he was straddling me, sixty-nining, his knees at my shoulders, and that wonderful, hot, thick, come-filled cock of his was brushing against my lips.

"Suck it, Carol," he growled. "Take it in your mouth and suck me dry."

The smell of Scott's crotch filled my nostrils. He again spread my legs and buried his face in my slit. I parted my lips and kissed, open-mouthed, over the head of his cock. He was slippery and salty, leaking so wetly he slid into my mouth with no effort at all.

"Oh, fuck, yes," he gasped. He thrust his hips, nudging himself farther into my mouth. "Suck me." He moaned as I took him deeper.

The sensations fed straight into my pussy. I was barely aware of thrusting my ass up to him. He sank his finger into my pussy and started rubbing. Then his other hand moved, slick and searching, to brush against my anus—against, and in. I cried out, arching up to meet him.

"Come for me, Carol," he breathed, his tongue lashing me again. His penis slipped over the back of my tongue and I tipped my head back, opening myself to him. Then I closed my eyes and let the throbbing red heat of orgasm consume me. Scott's roar filled my ears as he bathed my tongue and the back of my throat with spurt after spurt of his rich, hot, sticky semen.

We were both wasted. Scott's still-hard cock slid over my lips as he pulled forward and collapsed on me, his ass in the air, his cock dripping strands of cum and saliva, his body heavy as he tried to take his weight onto his arms and chest.

"God, I love you," he groaned, his chest still heaving. "You are one fucking hot lay."

It was hard to laugh with him crushing me, but I managed.

Eventually, our breathing returned to normal. I could feel Scott smiling as he turned and kissed the side of my leg with a loud smack. "If the rest of those jerks got blown like this, maybe we could get some work done in this town." He wrapped his arms around me and hugged fiercely. "Take us home, Ralph."

As the engine started, I leaned over and kissed the now-softened penis that rested so invitingly against his thigh. "It would be a helluva media campaign, lover boy."

Scott and I were still cuddling as we pulled back onto the expressway. Even through the glass, we heard Ralph laughing, saying, "You got my vote!"

# MOM'S NIGHT OUT

## Lolita Lopez

R elax," Owen urged, sliding his arms around my waist and pulling me back against his chest. The light stubble covering his cheek rasped my skin as he dipped his face and nuzzled his nose in the curve of my throat. "The kids are fine."

"I'm trying," I insisted, my nerves on edge. "It's hard to flip the mommy switch off, you know? I've been on call twenty-four/seven for the last fourteen months. Going from sippy cup duty to sexy night out with my husband isn't as easy as I'd thought it would be."

Owen's big, strong arms squeezed me tighter. He kissed my bare collarbone. "I know, sugar. But," he added carefully, "you need this night off, okay? You deserve a break. Besides, I'm sure my mom and your sister have it under control."

My lower lip wobbled and my stomach churned. "But what if—"

Before I could finish the thought, he gently turned me around in his arms and claimed my mouth. "Sh," he whispered softly.

"My mother was an ER nurse for thirty-plus years. Your sister is a pediatrician." He smiled and cupped my face, his thumb stroking my cheek. "I think the kids are going to be okay." His lips brushed mine again and I melted into his warm embrace. God, it had been so fucking long since we'd been able to kiss or hug without the constant fear of interruption. My admittedly irrational fears subsided as Owen's hands slipped under the fluffy white robe and caressed my naked skin. He was right. The kids were perfectly safe.

And I did deserve this. We deserved this night of uninterrupted lovemaking and relaxation. The last few years had been so difficult and stressful. Unsuccessful fertility treatments, a failed adoption, a surprise twin pregnancy and a solid adoption lead we couldn't abandon.

We'd gone from no kids to three newborns in the span of ten months. It had been nonstop craziness since the day we'd brought little Georgina home from the hospital to join her four-week-old brothers. Round the clock breastfeeding and pumping and mixing up formula to supplement. Kiddos who refused to sleep through the night. Teething, fevers, ear infections. Adjusting to a work-at-home schedule after my unexpected layoff.

Somehow we'd survived the first year. Things were finally slowing down and our routine was falling into place. Owen had been asking for a weekend away from the wild chaos of the house for weeks, but I'd fought him tooth and nail. Mommy guilt was a real bitch and put such a damper on things.

But a few nights back while slapping around for a lost pacifier in the dark, I'd had this profound moment of clarity. Going away for a night to recharge and reconnect didn't make me a terrible mother. It actually made me a damn good mama. I couldn't give the kiddos my very best if I wasn't feeling my very best.

So babysitting arrangements were made and a room was booked and off we went to a suite downtown for dinner and sex. Lots of sex. Lots of hot, kinky, dirty sex, the kind we'd enjoyed before kids. The kind we were too damn tired and modest to have at home. Nothing put a stop to wicked-hot, tear-the-sheets-from-the bed, knock-over-lamps sex like a wail from the nursery.

"God, I've missed this." Owen groaned as his hands drifted over my bare bottom and gave my plump cheeks a squeeze. A thrill of excitement rocked my core. I pressed against his chest, my breasts aching and nipples pulled tight. My hands reached for his head, my fingers sifting through his short hair. The thick soft cotton surrounding my body trapped heat close to my skin. I rubbed against him in near desperation to be rid of the plush garment.

"Take this off," he whispered gruffly, his hands already shoving the robe down my arms. It fell around my feet and I quickly kicked it away, my lips never leaving his mouth. Owen's tongue darted between my lips and swiped mine. I playfully bit the tip of his tongue before sucking it sensually. A rumble of pleasure vibrated right out of Owen's chest and into me. His hands fisted tightly in my still-damp hair as he devoured my mouth, his kisses deep and loving.

Like a starving man, he sought his sustenance from my lips, our wildly passionate kisses nourishing his long-neglected affections. Try as I might, I could never be everything to everyone. Embracing the role of devoted, loving mother often meant I collapsed in an exhausted heap at the end of the day. There wasn't always a lot of energy left over for Owen. Most nights, he did the same thing, flopping into bed beside me and passing out after we exchanged quick kisses.

Hell, one night, we'd both dozed off in the middle of vanilla missionary sex! I'd woken up with a start when Owen's weight crushed the air from my lungs. We'd laughed it off the next morning but it definitely drove the point home. We needed to make our relationship a priority again. Scheduling sex had improved the situation somewhat but sneaking in a quickie during naptime wasn't enough.

But this? Oh, god, *this* was exactly what we needed.

I grasped the front of the towel secured around Owen's waist and yanked hard. His stiff cock sprung free and jutted into my belly. I wrapped my fingers around his pulsing shaft and stroked the long, thick length. He shuddered and pressed his forehead to mine, his panting breaths buffeting my cheek.

I swiped my tongue along his lower lip before dropping to my knees. I nuzzled my face in the crease of his thigh and moved to his dick. The ruddy tip begged for attention. I let my wet tongue slither along the underside of the crown before sucking the head between my lips. Owen groaned and pushed the hair away from the sides of my face. He loved watching me suck his cock, so I made sure to put on quite the show.

I swirled my tongue around his shaft every time he pulled back and left it flat against the bottom of my mouth when he plunged deep. I worked the first few inches with my tongue and lips before taking him deeper and deeper into my throat. My hands moved to his hips, our silent signal that let him know I wanted him to fuck my mouth. His fingers tightened in my hair, the slight burning pain along my scalp sending a shock of excitement right to my clit. I loved it rough and a little kinky.

Jaw relaxed, I welcomed his thrusting cock. The squelching sound of his penis sliding in and out of my wet mouth made me so hot. My clit throbbed and I slid a hand down my naked belly and parted the cleanly shaven lips of my pussy. My fingers found my clit and rubbed the little nub.

I sensed Owen wouldn't last much longer. It had been so long since he'd fucked my face with such abandon. We were both on edge, the sexual tension strung taut between us. His breaths were short and fast. His fingers flexed against my scalp. He pulled out and stroked his hand down the glistening length of his cock, his skin shiny with my saliva.

"Come in my mouth," I begged, my heart racing with anticipation. "I want to taste your come."

Growling, Owen drove his cock deep. I bobbed on his shaft, using my tongue to stimulate that little spot on the underside of the head that drove him crazy. His fingers bit into my shoulders as he held me in place and came hard. The first splash of hot cum hit my tongue. My thighs clenched and I strummed my clit faster. Owen jerked a few times as he enjoyed his climax. I flicked my tongue over the supersensitive head of his cock, making him tremble and moan.

He smiled down at me and lovingly caressed my face as his shaft slipped from my mouth. I held his smoky gaze as I swallowed his semen. Owen's eyes flashed and he dragged his thumb across my lower lip, gathering the drops of cum clinging to my pout. I licked his finger clean and scraped my teeth over the pad of his thumb. He gave a little laugh and hauled me up to stand in front of him. His rough kiss stole the breath from my lungs.

I gasped when he grabbed the backs of my thighs and lifted me from the ground. "Owen! Put me down! I'm too big. You'll hurt your back!"

"Hush," he gently admonished and kissed my neck. "You're not too big." He gave my backside a squeeze. "You're just right."

If he hadn't been holding me up, I'd have melted into a puddle of goo at his feet. Leave it to Owen, my ridiculously ripped and drop-dead sexy husband, to make me feel beautiful despite the extra pounds on my plump frame.

He tossed me onto the mattress like a caveman and fell to his knees at the foot of the bed. Grabbing my waist, he hauled me down to the edge. I shivered when his hands touched my inner thighs and spread me wide open for his enjoyment. He pressed a kiss to the top of my mound and petted my sex. "Can't wait to taste your sweet cunt."

There was no mistaking the hunger in his voice. I closed my eyes and focused on the sensation of his fingers exploring me. He traced my slit, dipping his finger into me and then moving back up to my clit. My slick juices coated his skin and eased his movements.

"God, baby, you're so wet." He slipped two fingers inside my pussy and thrust slowly. "Does sucking my cock make you hot?"

"Yes." I shuddered as his tongue flicked side to side over my clit. I was so close to coming. I tried to hold my breath in the hopes of staving off the impending climax.

Owen seemed to sense my predicament. His tongue abandoned my clit and traced my folds. When his tongue replaced his fingers, I cried out and grabbed the comforter on either side of me. Squeezing the fabric in my fists, I rocked my hips as Owen held tight to my thighs and tongue-fucked my pussy. His nose rubbed against my clit, causing little shocks of pleasure to zing right through me. It was crazy good and I couldn't get enough.

His fingers were inside me again, three this time, pumping at a wild pace. His lips settled over my clit. He sucked hard, the suction boosting the tingling heat and sending my pulse into overdrive. When his tongue fluttered against my clit, I lost it. "I'm coming. Oh, god. Oh, *god*! Unnhh. Owen!"

Head thrown back, I called out his name again and again

as powerful wave after wave of pleasure crashed over me. That fabulously talented tongue of his knew just the right way to flick, just the right rhythm to keep my orgasm rolling. His fingers moved inside me, rubbing against my G-spot, as he forced a second orgasm quick on the heels of the first.

Before I could even catch my breath, Owen was on the bed and grabbing me by the waist. Swift and smooth, he flipped me onto my belly and pulled me up onto my knees. My belly flip-flopped. I loved it when Owen was impatient and behaved like a Neanderthal. It felt so fucking good to know my man wanted me that badly, that he had to have me *right now*.

Owen grasped my hips and shoved my knees apart. "Get me wet," he ordered gruffly, the deep timbre of his voice making me shake with anticipation.

I reached between my legs and found his throbbing cock. I dragged the head through my slick pussy lips, letting my slippery juices coat his skin. I pressed the tip to my entrance and dropped my hand to the mattress before I pushed back, fully sheathing his cock in my cunt. We both groaned: me from the sensation of fullness and Owen from the sensation of being balls deep in my hot, wet depths.

"Fuck me," I begged wantonly. "Fuck me hard."

Owen gave me exactly what I wanted. His fingers clamped around my waist as he jackhammered my pussy. Every jarring thrust sent shock waves of pleasure through my womb. He grabbed a handful of my hair and yanked. Teeth bared, I grunted and reached back to claw the side of his thigh.

"Are you my dirty whore?" He slapped my ass, the stinging pain spreading through my bottom like wildfire.

The thrill of such dirty talk and spanking made my head spin. I was practically delirious with lust. "Yes! Yes! Oh, god, yes."

*Smack. Smack. Smack.*

"Take it, Sidney. Take my cock."

"Give it to me, Owen. I want it all."

Seconds later, I felt Owen's spit-slicked fingers probing my anus. My eyelids drifted together as I enjoyed the naughty little thrill of having my ass played with while my husband fucked me senseless. Anal sex wasn't something we engaged in very often. It was a delicacy in our house, something to be savored when it was offered every few weeks.

The sensation of double penetration felt so fucking good. I reached down between my legs and rubbed my clit. It was still sensitive from the orgasms Owen had given me but I didn't care. I wanted to come again. I wanted to come with Owen's cock in my pussy and his fingers twisting in my ass. I flicked my wrist faster and faster, increasing the pressure of my fingertips as I chased what promised to be a mind-blowing climax.

Utter filth spilled from Owen's beautiful mouth, the words driving me insane. I was hearing all those dirty, smutty things I loved so much but was too embarrassed to request at home now. He spanked my big ass hard, his flat palm leaving streaks of heat on my olive skin. I pushed back against him, meeting his thrusts and rolling my hips.

We were wild with lust. The bed shook with the force of our frenzied mating. The sheets stood no chance and popped from the mattress, the elastic too weak to withstand our passionate fucking. Somewhere in the back of my mind I knew we were loud, maybe too loud, and were probably disturbing the occupants in the rooms below and on either side of us.

But I didn't care. I'd been holding it in for so long, too long. I'd been forced to smother the urge to shout obscenities and cry out in ecstasy. This was my night to let loose. I'd earned this. I deserved this.

We exploded just seconds apart, me first and Owen not far behind. I gushed around his cock as he hammered deep and fast. My G-spot buzzed and my clit throbbed. The intensity of my climax knocked the breath from my lungs. I couldn't even call out his name. I could only shake and gyrate as my cunt spasmed and the pleasurable bursts rocked my body.

Owen thrust deep, the force pushing me forward onto the mattress. He gave a few shallow pumps as he ejaculated and then collapsed against me in a sweaty heap. A few moments later, he rolled off onto his back. My body felt suddenly empty as my pussy and ass contracted with aftershocks. I draped myself across Owen and hooked my leg over his thigh.

A low rumble rattled in his chest and vibrated my cheek. He stroked my hair as he laughed. In a state of pure elation, I caught the giggles from him. Like a couple of fools, we laughed ourselves silly.

"Jesus," he swore breathlessly. "That was amazing."

"I know." I exhaled loudly. "The best in a long, long time." My body hummed with the delicious warmth of afterglow. I snuggled close to Owen and enjoyed his gentle caresses. "You were right, you know. About taking a night away from the kids," I clarified. "We needed this."

"Hold on," he said, a teasing smile curving his lips. "Let me grab my phone and jot this down on the calendar."

I playfully smacked his arm. "Behave."

"No, really. How often do I hear that from you?"

"Probably not as often as you should," I admitted.

Still grinning, he cupped my cheek and tilted my face up toward his. "I love you, Sidney."

"I know." I smiled and kissed his chin. "I'm pretty fond of you, too." He snorted and ruffled my hair. "But, really, I love you, Owen. Like. A lot."

We lapsed into a comfortable silence. I drew lazy circles on his chest. "We should do this more often."

"What?" He laughed. "Run away from home?"

I nodded and kissed his cheek. "Exactly."

# SLOW FIRE

## Donna George Storey

D el was expecting the good-night kiss. For weeks, Shelby had been ending their dates at her door with an embrace and a gentle, almost reverent brush of his lips against hers. She was completely taken by surprise, however, when he cut the engine midway up the private drive to her family's house, leaned over, and *possessed* her with a kiss, his tongue gliding between her lips. This kiss was graceful, teasing, patient, as if he did nothing all day but sit around and kiss a woman instead of doing his filial duty as an associate at his father's law firm.

She was the first to pull away. It took a moment to catch her breath.

"I hope I didn't overstep?" The concern in his voice reassured her that he was—that knee-buckling kiss to the contrary—the Shelby she knew, a man who was perhaps a little too proper and cautious.

She laughed. "Oh, no. It was a nice trip down memory lane."

He laughed, too, obviously relieved. "You taught me how to French kiss that night, you know."

"Did I? I guess you always did do well at your lessons." Del thought back on that evening, more than eight years ago. Although they'd never dated, somehow Shelby ended up driving her home from one of the countless parties for the graduates of the class of '56. Somehow they ended up parking and kissing, just kissing, until well past midnight. And though Shelby would never know this, when she'd gotten home she was so restless, she somehow ended up putting her hand between her legs to calm the strange, hot itch down there and climaxed for the very first time.

For a long moment they sat in silence.

Del wished he would kiss her again.

Instead he said, "When can I see you again?"

She smiled. "What did you have in mind?"

"Are you free tomorrow after church?"

"The busybodies will wonder about your intentions." She'd meant to be flirtatious, but immediately regretted the words.

He took her hand and squeezed it. "Some of them already are wondering. I assure you my intentions are most honorable."

Her stomach tightened. Shelby was a perfect catch. She, on the other hand, was damaged goods, more damaged than anyone in this fine, upstanding town suspected. But she was used to putting a brave face on her troubles. "Would you like to go hiking around Windy Knoll tomorrow afternoon? I'm sure my mother would be delighted to have you stay for supper."

"I'd love that," he said with a smile. He turned the key in the ignition. With a sinking feeling, she realized there would be no more kisses tonight. When they reached the house, Shelby jumped out of the car, came around to her door and opened it for her. On the porch, he made his customary chaste good-bye.

Once inside, Del peeped through the window and watched the rear lights of his Thunderbird recede down the wooded lane.

She was feeling anything but chaste now.

Del lay in bed in the darkness, willing herself to resist the *urge*. Once, when she was much younger, she'd overheard some crude men in town discussing a widow and her "needs," which they all seemed most willing to satisfy. Del didn't quite understand what they meant, but their sly, oily voices made her blush. Now she did understand. She wanted to be with a man tonight so desperately, she thought she might jump out of her skin. Not exactly Shelby, although his kiss lingered on her lips, between her thighs. Yet she still couldn't yet reconcile the comfort she felt in his presence with these darker longings.

She certainly wasn't thinking of her late husband. She'd once been crazy in love with Bill, a brilliant—and twice-divorced—jazz pianist twenty years her senior. She'd met him at the music conservatory where he occasionally taught students who had the courage to venture beyond Mozart. Bill turned out to be a charismatic teacher outside the rehearsal room as well, a veritable expert in the secret music of the flesh. She eloped with him a month after they met, the subject of raised eyebrows and scandalized whispers in Del's hometown. She had plenty of time to repent the impulsive move. She and her mother had already consulted with a lawyer about a divorce on grounds of adultery and desertion when she heard the news Bill had been in a fatal car accident somewhere outside New York.

No, the man she chose to be with tonight didn't have a particular face or name. He was every man all mixed together in a heady cocktail guaranteed to satisfy a hot-blooded widow. He had Bill's wickedly seductive voice, Shelby's scent of Old

Spice, the fingers of the father of one of her piano students, which were so thick and sturdy she couldn't help but imagine them stroking her until her female juices flowed.

Ah, he was here now, to fill her every depraved need. All she had to do was obey.

"Lift up your nightgown so I can see you, Del. You want to show yourself to me, don't you?"

*Yes.*

She always said yes to this man, no matter what he asked. Slowly, she inched the flannel nightgown up over her hips, up and up until she was fully exposed.

"Ah, look at those lovely breasts. So sensitive, all I have to do is tweak your nipple and you'll swoon in my arms. Just a few minutes of kissing and fondling those pretty tits, and you'll do anything for me, won't you? That's how I first taught you to take me in your mouth. Most well-bred girls won't do such naughty things, Del, but you were so very willing. Because you like the way it feels, don't you?"

*Yes.*

As if by magic, Del's mouth flooded with the taste of him, salt and musk and male secrets.

"Touch your breasts, Del. I know it gets you all wet down there. I like to see you all wet and swollen and ready."

Blushing, she dutifully licked her fingers and began to twist her stiff pink nipples.

"Very good. Now, while you're rubbing your pretty tits, I want you to tell me what you like to do with a man. Don't mumble the words. Articulate. When we name our desires, we're halfway to fulfilling them."

Del whimpered. Like a teacher drilling a student, Bill used to tease his innocent bride into saying dirty words out loud in bed—*cock, pussy, screw.*

"I like to suck cocks," she whispered.

"Indeed. And what else, my naughty darling?"

"I like to screw. I like to screw so much, I did it before I was married."

"That's right. You let an older man lure you to his apartment and take full advantage of you. You are so very wicked. Now tell me what wicked thing you want to do tonight."

Del swallowed hard. "I want to make love to myself while... while you watch."

The man chuckled. "I'm watching."

Del slipped her finger between her soft folds and began to strum.

"That's right. All the men in town are watching you now, Del. They know you're a lascivious young widow with *needs*. Tell them you'll suck their cocks, first come, first served. Because you find big, hard cocks *irresistible*. Or maybe you'd rather screw all of them in the gazebo in the town square? They line up around the block and take you from behind, one after the other, until your thighs are dripping with their seed. Such a bad, bad girl you are."

Del choked back a moan. Her crisis was near. She was so wet, her finger made a sucking sound as it worked her sweet spot. With her other hand, she began to pinch her nipple desperately, as if she were plucking the strings of a violin. The last lewd image flashing into her head was of Shelby unzipping his fly; freeing a thick, red cock; pressing it between her lips. *Take this in your mouth. Suck me until I come.*

And so she came, her hips jerking rhythmically into the mattress, one tiny squeak of a moan leaking from her lips.

Panting and spent, she pulled down her gown and curled up under the blanket. She was never quite sure what possessed her on nights like this. Would Shelby still court her if he knew about the unspeakable, decadent things her fevered brain concocted? On the other hand, if she played her cards right, she might well tempt him into kissing her again tomorrow.

Smiling, Del drifted into a satisfied sleep.

When they reached the crest of the hill, the sun was already setting, veils of amber, ocher and mauve stretched across the horizon.

"You can see all the way to the next county from here," she told him, her voice slightly winded from the climb.

Shelby moved close, almost, but not quite, touching her. "It's a beautiful spot."

"I used to come up here almost every day when I first moved back home. That was in November, too. In the summer, the hills seem to catch fire as the sun sets, but at this time of year it's more like a glow that rises up from the land itself then fades, so gently you almost miss it."

"Like a slow fire," he murmured.

"Yes. Slow fire. I like that." She looked up at him and smiled.

He cleared his throat and looked off into the distance. "Have you ever thought of marrying again?"

Her pulse quickened. With expectation or dread, she wasn't quite sure.

"I might, under the right conditions," she replied cautiously.

He cleared his throat again. "I'm not doing this properly. I should get down on bended knee with a ring, but might I hope that I could offer you those conditions some day? I'm not in a rush. I just wanted to declare my intentions. You know you mean everything to me, Del."

She felt a click in her chest, as if a tiny lock had opened. The words came out before she could stop herself. "Oh, Shelby, I want to say yes."

He laughed, relief mixed with amusement. "Then why not say it?"

At a loss, she threw her arms around him. She didn't want him to see the tears in her eyes. There was so much he didn't know about her. Living with a man changed a woman, marked her indelibly body and soul, not always for the better. If only they could spend the night together before they rushed into marriage, to make sure this wasn't mere lust or wishful thinking.

Suddenly it hit her. Why couldn't they be together? She was, after all, a widow with nothing to lose. And if it didn't work out, best to know now and save each other years of heartache.

"I do have one condition. Or maybe it's a favor," she said into the air over his shoulder.

"I'll do anything you ask," he replied.

Would he? She brought her lips to his ear, as if someone might overhear. "Before I can say yes, I want us to be together. Intimately. To see if we're compatible."

He inhaled sharply. Then there was silence. An endless silence. Her cheeks flaming with shame, Del shook herself free and began walking quickly back toward the house.

In a few strides, he was beside her. "Don't go, Del. Of course I'll do it, if you're sure you want that."

She stopped, her eyes still trained on the withered winter grass at her feet.

"I'd be very honored to make love to you," he said.

She bit her lip. Rather than shocked or disgusted, he actually sounded eager. Her blush deepened. "You'll have to find a place. We can't have anyone find out. And we'll have to take precautions."

"Of course. I'll take care of everything." He paused, his head tilted in thought. "We can use my family's hunting cabin. If we leave in the morning, we can be back by nightfall. We'll say we're hiking the Blue Ridge."

It was a clever plan.

"Shelby? Do you think I'm a bad woman?"

"No, Del. I think you're a wise one."

When he kissed her this time, it was even slower and sweeter than the night before.

Shelby called the cabin "primitive," but Del found the place cozy. While she unpacked the picnic, he set about making a fire in the wood-burning stove. As the bedrooms had no direct heat, they carried a mattress into the living room. Shelby apologized many times for putting her to work.

"I don't mind. It's like camping."

In fact, there was almost a childish, holiday giddiness between them as they made up the bed together with sheets he'd bought at a Woolworths in another town so as not to raise suspicions. At Shelby's suggestion, they kicked off their shoes and picnicked on the mattress with Virginia ham and biscuits, apples from the Windy Knoll orchard, slices of Del's mother's spice cake.

As they ate, a steady rain began to fall.

"I'm glad we're not really hiking right now," she said.

"I can't tell you how glad I am we're not really hiking right now." He took her hand and kissed the tip of each finger. The last one, her pinkie, he sucked all the way into his hot, satiny mouth.

She gasped at his audacity. He'd already made her wet.

He drew her toward him and leaned back onto the mattress so they lay entwined, like a couple that had just made love. She felt his heart beating faintly through his sweater.

"Before we...well, first I have something to say to you, Del."

Her stomach did a somersault. He sounded worried, even afraid.

"What is it?"

"I wanted to tell you that, well, I've never gone all the way before. I know a lot of men go with a professional for their first time. That never seemed right to me. But right now I almost wish I had. Then I could make love to you better today."

Warmth flooded her chest. How sweet of him to worry about impressing her. And how very different from Bill, who'd had dozens of women before her and just as many after. "Oh, Shelby, this isn't a test for you. It's about me. You're so decent and pure, and you know my marriage wasn't exactly a success."

"You have no reason to blame yourself for what happened, Del," he insisted.

"I know it was partly his nature, but he grew tired of me so quickly. I could feel it happen. He'd look right through me, as if I wasn't even there." She faltered. Oddly, this confession felt more private than making love.

He tightened his arm around her. "It must have been hard for you. But I'm not like that. I'll be good to you."

"I know you'll be good to me. I'm not sure why that scares me so much. I guess I'm afraid I'll do it wrong."

He pressed his lips to her hair. "Oh, baby, don't worry for a minute. You and I will figure out how to do it right together. And I wanted to tell you something else. I've kissed a few other girls in my time, and not one came close to you. I know we have something special."

"Yes," she said. "I think maybe we do."

"Give me another lesson today. Teach me the way you want it to be."

Del caught her breath. Yet she had to stop and think—how did she want it to be?

She wanted it slow and lovely, the slow fire of the earth rising to meet the sun.

"Kiss me first. Kiss me until we can't bear it anymore."

And so they kissed. As if they had all the time in the world. They kissed until Del couldn't tell where her lips ended and his began, until his scent and saliva filled her mouth, until her breasts felt unbearably achy and in need of hands to soothe them.

"May I undress you now?" he whispered. As if he knew it was time.

*Yes.*

Slowly, he unbuttoned her blouse, reached around to unsnap her brassiere. He let out an, "Oh," when he saw her bare breasts. He seemed almost afraid to touch them.

She took his hand and brought it to her breast. "I'm sensitive there. Be gentle at first, just kisses and caresses. Later you can be rougher."

With a soft grunt of assent, he bent to take her nipple in his mouth. Instinctively, he cupped her other breast, his thumb flicking her nipple lightly.

When he had her whimpering and squirming, he slowly unzipped her skirt and helped her wriggle out of her girdle and stockings. He stroked her stomach and thighs. Finally his hand came to rest between her legs.

*Yes.*

She parted her thighs.

His finger dipped between her lips. "It's like satin. So soft. Show me. Show me how to please you."

*Yes.*

Del moaned. He wanted to see her pleasure. And she wanted to show him.

Sliding her hand under his, she touched her middle finger to her most sensitive spot. Shelby's hand remained poised above hers, as if it were listening, studying her response. Then he gently nudged hers aside and began to stroke her.

"Is this all right?"

*Yes.*

She arched back into the mattress. She let him pleasure her until her legs trembled and her secret muscles clenched rhythmically in their hunger.

"It's time. Did you bring a rubber?"

"Yes, right here." Shelby reached into his back pocket. Through the veil of her lashes, she watched him quickly undress. She noted that his cock was of a good size, shorter than Bill's but thicker, and flushed a delicious, deep red. She longed to suck it, but thought it best to save *that* lesson for later. Shelby lay back and rolled on the prophylactic rather awkwardly, then turned to her.

"I'm yours, Del."

He was, wasn't he? She would be his first in this, too.

"Lie still," she whispered. "You can hold out better that way."

He nodded, lips pursed, like an earnest schoolboy.

Filled with love for him, Del straddled his broad stomach.

She'd never heard such a sound of pure pleasure as when he glided inside her.

It felt good for her, too, so good after all this time, to have the rigid length of him pressing up into her belly. She rocked against him, rubbing her sweet spot over the coarse hairs at the base of his cock. He grimaced. She could tell he was doing his very best to hold back, so she took it slow, tucking her feet under his thighs to intensify the pressure. Before long her hips seemed to take on a will of their own, thrusting faster and faster.

*Yes.*

This was good. Very good. She could feel her climax gather at the base of her spine, burst into flame and shoot up into her skull.

*Yes.*

She cried out, jerking into him with each spasm. Shelby grabbed her buttocks and began to pump up into her, until he, too, cried out.

She collapsed over him, her chest slick with sweat. They held each other for a long time.

"I think I've died and gone to heaven, Del."

"I think I have my answer for you."

"Does that mean you'll say yes?"

"I already said yes to you about a hundred times just now. Weren't you listening?" she teased.

"How do you feel about a Christmas wedding? I can't wait any longer."

"I thought you liked to take it slow."

"Eight years isn't slow enough for you?"

She laughed.

He kissed her then, long and slow and sweet. A memory and a beginning.

# THE NUDE, STRIPPED NAKED

## Jeremy Edwards

He wished everyone had indicator lights, akin to a taxi's roof-mounted mechanism, for inviting or warding off a stranger's attention. Patrick would have loved to know, without a shred of doubt, when his gaze on the ass of an attractive individual was or was not welcome.

*I shouldn't stare at a strange woman's ass, but it's okay to "notice" it, right?* He constantly struggled with the lines that divided *noticing, looking,* and *staring.* And this applied to faces as well as asses. He wished he could mount a podium someday and officially apologize to every stranger, past and future, who might have felt the scrape of his eyes when they lingered too long in a crosswalk or pub or museum.

Patrick wanted to be distant, where appropriate, and daring, where appropriate. He wished his libido and his conscience could sit down in a conference room, mark out the boundaries, then fax him a memo and a map.

"The buttocks lack definition," said Margie.

He started, his ruminations interrupted.

"I didn't want to stare," he explained.

"Patrick," said the teacher, with emphasis. "This is figure drawing class. She's your model."

The problem was that the nude model, a dark-haired vision of about thirty, was the most beautiful woman he'd ever seen, with or without clothes on. Beautiful, not simply in a "Wow, you should be an artist's model" sense (though she was exactly that), but in a flesh-sizzling, chemistry-sparking, all-he-wanted-to-do-was-fuck-her sense. Which wasn't even accurate—because fucking her wasn't *all* Patrick wanted to do. There was also nibbling her thighs, licking her pussy, slapping her ass, tickling her armpits...

But these were not things one did to a nude model. These were things one did to a naked woman.

And that was why looking at her at all felt like a transgression—because Patrick was unable to look at her without it being sexual, rather than artistic. His assessment of her shoulder was drenched in a lascivious appreciation for how admirably its shape would satisfy his mouth. His appraisal of her waist, though it drew on the clinical eye for proportion that Margie had helped her students develop, was wired to a groin-deep desire to clutch her in that perfect concavity with one hand while reverently exploring her cunt with the other. And to look at his model's derriere with anything but jeans-straining want—to look, especially, at the base of the cheek where it winked into the crack, hinting at the deeper, richer crevice nestled within—was an impossibility.

And yet, though her face blended a soft serenity with an angular brightness and her petite breasts looked ripe and full presiding over her small swell of tummy, and the triangle of fur at the juncture of her legs had a luxurious sheen, it was the whole, more than the parts, that forbade Patrick to remain detached. She embodied something that he could not name but which he desired to know, hold and feast upon.

Objectively, he could see that the bland lighting of the classroom had a tendency to make flesh mimic marble—that to the other students, the model probably looked timeless rather than present, immortal rather than alive. Just as she was supposed to. Objectively, Patrick recognized that it should have been challenging to imagine her face broken up by laughter...her fingertips drumming restlessly on a tabletop...her warm, gaping pussy greeting the morning with fresh pee. Nonetheless, he could imagine all this—indeed could not help but imagine it.

And after he'd been sketching another quarter hour under Margie's distant but firm supervision, he began to get the impression that his gaze was affecting his model, despite the fact that she couldn't see him watching her. As he drew, her skin seemed to morph from vanilla to the palest pink champagne; and though the studio lights were no more nor less hot than they'd been all session, he now discovered a sparkle of perspiration on her shoulder blades. At one point, when she shifted her position minutely, almost imperceptibly, Patrick felt that it meant the difference between repose and autoerotica...that her thighs were now conscious of each other, and of what they enclosed.

"Margie?" He practically whispered it, lest he disturb the exquisite figure.

The instructor walked to Patrick's station, cocking an eyebrow to ask what he needed.

"What's the model's name?" This time he did whisper.

"Why?"

He shrugged, squirming inside with the awkwardness of the situation, but determined nonetheless. "I feel I'll be able to capture her better if I know her name," he said slyly. Ridiculously.

"A minute ago, you were afraid to look at her."

He stared optimistically at his unfinished drawing.

"Her name is Nicola."

It was hard to tell, with Nicola's face turned three-quarters away from the class, but Patrick thought she smiled.

He realized, in the days that followed, that he was obsessed with her. *Obsessed,* he told himself, almost proudly. It was something more elemental and profound than the usual infatuation, and it made him feel pathetic and grand all at once.

In the yearning throes of masturbation, he felt as if he wanted to be her—as well as himself—while pounding into her: to experience both halves, to get a privileged glimpse into the state of mind of a nude who was being fucked—by him. He felt greedy, narcissistic and yet generous; he wanted to share it all with her, make her blazingly wet between her naked legs, make her scream shrilly with pleasure, proving to all the world that her throat was raw, sensuous velvet, and not marble.

There was no mistaking that the woman in the high-necked button-down sweater, standing by one of the campus statues with her coffee, was Nicola.

Patrick stopped, a short but safe distance away, to say a good-morning, articulating her name for the umpteenth time that day—but the first time aloud. "You might recognize me from art class," he added tactfully.

"Of course. You're Perry—no, sorry...um, *Patrick. Patrick?*"

Her misstep and her uncertainty soothed his jitters, as did the anarchic motion of her stray hairs in the wind. *She looks more like twenty-nine now than thirty,* he said to himself. He knew this was a stupid way to think about it, but at twenty-one, he was a little frightened of women who had attained the presumed perfection of their thirties and beyond.

He nodded. "Yeah, it's Patrick. You must be waiting for somebody."

"No," said Nicola. Then she grinned. "My date is already here."

She put her arm around the waist of Isaac Danton, LLD, a college founder who had been immortalized in concrete—and whose obligatory stiffness further accented Nicola's vitality. Patrick observed that even in the midst of a spontaneous, comical gesture, with a cardboard cup in hand, Nicola's poise was heavenly.

He laughed gratefully at her friendly antics.

"But seriously," she said. "I'm just taking a break. I like standing here with my coffee—it's the crossroads of our little world, isn't it?"

He glanced around. "I see what you mean." Then he looked straight at Professor Danton, avoiding Nicola's eye. "I wish I had a coffee, so I could stand here."

She beckoned him over. "Please. You've already proved yourself better company than Danton. And the coffee is optional."

Encouraged, Patrick became bold. He joined her, at ease now with himself and his actions.

"Can I ask you something?" he said, after a beat.

"Sure."

"What was it like the first time you got...nude in front of an artist?" He wanted to know how a flesh-and-blood human beauty transformed herself into pure, bare art.

She blushed. "Wow, when you ask me something, you really ask me something."

"I'm sorry."

"No, it's okay. It's an interesting question." She took a sip of coffee. "I guess—I guess it was sort of strange. Not because I was nervous—I wasn't, really—but because it thrilled me a bit. In just the way the philistines always like to imagine nude models get...amorous, to use a genteel word."

She raised her eyebrows. Patrick's fingers sweated in the pockets of his denim jacket, though not from anxiety now.

Nicola continued. "I worried that this meant I had an 'unprofessional attitude' but I couldn't help it. It wasn't even a question of being attracted to the artist I was modeling for. It was just the fact of exposing myself in such a formal manner. It was different from all the other ways I'd been naked before. So—ta-da!—you're speaking to a card-carrying exhibitionist."

Patrick was tingling all over, feverishly visualizing "all the ways" Nicola had been naked. "Wow. When you answer me something, you really answer."

"Exhibitionists are good at that."

He met her gaze. "I have the same problem. I get, uh, *unprofessional* inside, in art class. Well, lately I do."

Her eyes flickered with the fire of interest. "I know."

Despite his burgeoning confidence, the tension paralyzed him here. But Nicola cut through it by kissing him, right there at the elbow of Professor Danton. And just as he was getting used to her warm lips, so curious for his responses, he felt the grope of a small, frisky tongue. A tongue that uttered, nonverbally, the word *more*.

"I've finished my coffee," she said, prying his fingers out of his left pocket.

"Where are we going?" She'd begun walking, without relinquishing her light grip on his hand.

"I don't know. Where were you going before you saw me by the statue?"

"I don't know. I hadn't decided."

She laughed.

"How about you? You said you were taking a break," he recalled. "From what?"

"I don't know. I hadn't decided." She broke into a frivolous run, looking back to make sure he was chasing along behind her.

He caught up easily and grabbed her, daring to let her bottom feel his hardness. "You were much more subdued in the art studio."

"Rambunctious models aren't in high demand. And giggling models risk getting ejected."

He squeezed her harder and spoke directly to the teases of ear that were visible through her hair. "I'm glad you weren't ejected." He tickled her midriff, turning her, briefly, into a giggling model.

They ambled on, until Nicola paused in front of the music library. "Do you mind if we stop in here for a second?"

He followed her as she found her way to the bound sheet-music collections she needed. Her hips, lovely but unassuming in her indigo denim, conveyed a subtle rhythmic liveliness as she navigated the aisles.

"People assume that because I model, I'm in the art program," she explained when they were back outside. "But I'm a PhD candidate in music, who's merely posing as an art person. Literally."

"So there's no point trying to seduce you into painting me."

"Nope. You'll have to think of something else to seduce me into."

"You mean like composing a sonata about me?"

"No way. You couldn't possibly sit still that long."

Not with her around, he couldn't.

* * *

"Are we going to have another kiss?" She had invited him into her apartment.

He held her shoulders while he did it, letting his tongue fondle her contours as hers had his. "Yes," he said afterward, in belated reply to her query.

"I know you've seen me nude," Nicola said with a pretty quaver in her voice. "But would you like to see me naked?"

The sunlight in her kitchen was a lewd shade of yellow, so different from the academic fluorescence under which he'd previously observed her skin and her shape. And whereas Nicola the model had undressed behind a screen, to emerge in a robe that she shed impersonally upon posing, Nicola the private woman let Patrick see every intimate detail of the process: the way the third button of her jersey clung to the fabric lips that suckled it; the way her jeans required an extra yank to get past the luscious flare of her bottom; the way the elastic of her moist panties was digging in on one side, because of having worked themselves slightly off center in the course of the morning. The interplay of the living, bending, wriggling body with the garments appeared to Patrick as a sexual interaction in and of itself, an expression of carnal kineticism that was such a far cry from the isolated idealism of her form as presented to the art students.

He noticed that she had faint freckles on her chest, and he was sure they'd been invisible in the studio. So much had been bleached out there, he now realized, even to his transgressive gaze.

And now the naked woman did something else that the nude model had not: she touched herself. It was the same bare flesh that Patrick had seen in art class...but now Nicola's hands sculpted the weight of her breasts and stroked the pout of her pussy. Now Nicola's body told him that she wanted to be, not studied and sketched, but fingered, fondled, and fucked.

She brought a pussy-dipped finger to his mouth. He was so dizzy with excitement that he couldn't really taste the flavor. He could only taste the electricity.

"I'm going to go out on a limb—or at least a thigh—and suggest we visit my bedroom," said Nicola.

He tried to undress himself for her, but her precise, quiet touch was all over him. His shirt was history, then his pants. She covered his torso with kisses, and pulled his briefs to his trembling knees. His cock licked the palm of her hand.

In the hush of the late morning, Nicola sat on Patrick's face, and he nurtured her wiggling succulence until she slathered him, and slathered him again. Her sex-pink asscheeks, muffin sweet on his own cheeks, pressed down on him with animal lust, while her fingers made promises to his arching hips, his bouncing balls and his teetering rod.

As if paddling out to sea on a surfboard, she shimmied down his body from face to lap, mounting his cock with a grunt and a singing moan. The pleasure was so intense that he couldn't think, almost couldn't hear or see. He was barely aware of the mechanics by which Nicola was dragging and scraping herself up and down—how she milked him with slow meticulous-ness, inching her way, both literally and figuratively, toward a consummate tautness that would snap into a cloud of ecstasy.

When it snapped, and Nicola shrieked, he trained his eyes on the molten marble of her back, focusing on the arc of her spine until focus eluded him.

"I always wanted to make love to art." He kissed a nipple.

"*I* am not art, Patrick. A model is only food for thought."

"Mm...food." He settled his teeth around her elbow.

"You're the one who makes the art. You're the artist."

"Well, it's just a two-credit elective."

She cracked up into her pillow, her naked ass jiggling in the humble glow of the bedside lamp.

He was so glad it was okay to stare at it.

# EDGE

## Skylar Kade

M y lover came to me with one request—let him take the lead for a night. Though I was loath to give up control, the love shining in his eyes compelled me to say yes. Months of his gentle acquiescence to my quirks, my long hours and post-work terseness—I could do no less than give over the reins. But I didn't have to like it.

I drove to his farm that night with a white-knuckled grip, navigating the now-familiar roads with ease, though we usually met at my downtown condo that was closer to my office and he didn't once complain. Dislike of the unknown slithered around in my stomach, topped with my own disgust of having any reaction at all. My poker face won me money in Vegas and cases in the courtroom. I'd worn it so long it had become part of me.

He met me at the door with that familiar, gentle smile. The corners of my lips edged up in reply. His kiss told me he knew this wasn't easy. His feet, though, still guided me into his surprisingly luxurious bathroom. I'd always found the juxtaposition between hard outdoor labor and bathing in this temple to sensuality intriguing.

"Do you trust me?" he rumbled against my ear, his voice barely louder than the water running from the bathtub faucet.

I cleared my throat and swallowed past the lump that had settled there. "It's a little late for that, don't you think?"

Blindfolded, tied naked to a plastic chair in that huge Jacuzzi bathtub—hands behind my back, legs lashed to chair legs. Served me right for giving up control. How quickly he'd transformed from gentle horse breeder to fierce lover. A side of him I'd never before seen but was as counter to the man I'd known as his bathroom. It likewise pulled my attention and quickened my heart.

John looked unassuming, but underneath that Clark Kent exterior was a man whose deviancy could rival the mind of Lex Luthor, a side he'd kept well hidden until now. Lust and love had lit his eyes with eager arousal as he bound me; his hands, gentle as ever, soothed the goose bumps from my naked flesh. I'd seen his creativity and his passion, sure, but never like this. He'd been content letting me take charge in the bedroom—or the bathroom, as it were. Or so I'd thought.

His satisfied laugh vibrated down to my clitoris. My discomfort turned him on, his enjoyment turned me on, and we were stuck in this sensual loop until he got tired of it.

A thrill scuttled down my spine. He would end this, not I.

Having learned from past experience that his patience far outstripped mine, I tried to sink into the moment. It worked, until the air currents shifted and I knew he had left me there like a heroine tied to train tracks—only I didn't think any of those dames had wet pussies before they were saved.

A clink of metal on porcelain came from the expansive

vanity outside the main bathroom and my already overactive imagination jumped into hyperdrive. He returned on a whiff of good cologne and better pipe tobacco and I prayed the waiting was over.

"Keep your legs spread," he ordered. As I complied, goose bumps had their way with my skin until my flesh jumped with every exhale that skimmed across it. My pussy clenched in reaction, cool air drifting through my curls to barely swipe across my clit and chill the wetness coating my labia.

A warm washcloth stroked between my legs and I squirmed, feeling vulnerable and dirty. "I took a shower this morning," I groused.

He ruffled my hair as he always did when I bordered on ridiculous. "Your skin needs to be warm and wet."

I snorted. "Wet is right."

His hand cracked against my inner thigh and I gasped in shock. "Did you just hit me?"

"No, love, that was a spank." He did it again and the spot tingled and grew warm. I twitched and tried to close my legs only to feel the restraints press into my ankles, fighting as much against his torment as my own pleasure from it.

"Stop being a brat."

My next protest caught in my throat. I had this desperate need to please him, to be open and exposed and submissive. The usual me scorned the situation. I told the bitch to shut it. I craved something just out of my reach and somehow I knew he could bring it to me.

A soft kiss landed on my lips right before he devoured my mouth. And I let him, falling back under his crazy, unpredictable spell.

God, I loved him, even if it meant letting him have his way tonight.

I inhaled his comforting scent and he ran his hands across the long lines of my body once more, as if he were soothing one of his skittish colts. I calmed beneath him, as helpless under his command as those horses.

When cool foam hit my mound, his work-roughened fingers spreading it across the seam of my inner thighs, across my nether lips, around the hood of my clit, I knew what he had planned. Disappointment shadowed my excitement; I'd hoped for something more than grooming, something he'd oh-so-politely inquired about a few weeks earlier. I'd agreed and never gotten around to it.

I had wanted him to take me to the edge and tempt me to fall—or threaten to push me.

A soft metallic snick cut through my malaise and blood roared in my ears. It took me two tries before my throat wasn't as dry as the Arizona air. "What—"

"Do you trust me?" he asked again, this time pressing a fine, cool edge to my thigh, against my femoral artery.

I blame it on my addiction to crime shows but in that moment fear grabbed me in a stranglehold. He laughed—sinister—and I couldn't say the word. The blade trailed up, doing no more than denting the skin. No cut, no blood that I could feel.

A swish later and cool air danced across a formerly curl-covered section of my mound. I moaned, foamy flesh so dull in comparison to this new nakedness.

This, thrilling, dangerous, was what I needed. "Yes," I said, lust melting my insides until only my restraints kept me upright. The blade didn't return to my skin; I started to pant and twitch with anticipation.

Then it landed again. "Be still," his low, hard voice cautioned. "You don't want me to slip."

I froze despite my every molecule vibrating like they'd been hit by electricity. Those interminable minutes, the blade glossing across my most tender flesh while I fought to stay still beneath his skilled hands...I'd never been so aroused.

A now-cool washcloth skimmed across my now-naked pussy. I'd never been clean shaven, or shaved, for that matter. It was like all those sensitive nerves had been imprisoned. The antici- pation and wisps of air had me on the brink of orgasm.

And that was before his fingers went exploring. "Do not come without permission," he said.

I gasped in pleasure and indignation, unsure if I could obey but not caring about anything but his calloused fingertips tracing the lines of my labia. That cold bitch raised her serpen- tine head to protest such weakness, but I turned away from the offered apple.

Down one side, up the other, a swirl across my clit. "I'm going to come," I said, my voice rising with each word.

He pinched my sensitized mound. "Not yet." He continued his delicious torture and I fought off the rising pleasure by trying to recite closing arguments, recall details from legal briefs, hoping he'd give me permission soon. From deep inside, I needed to please him as much as he was pleasing me, and that meant obeying. The desire, struggle, bled onto my face and unused muscles awakened under my impending orgasm. My blood pounded in time to my silent mantra of, "Soon, soon."

I wouldn't disappoint him by coming without permission. I asked again.

One finger entered me and homed in on my G-spot with prac- ticed ease. My request devolved into incoherent jabber while pinpricks of pleasure jitterbugged with my spine.

"Say it like you mean it," his soft words dared.

I knew what he wanted. But I don't beg. Ever. My head shook back and forth, waffling almost as much as my instincts.

A second finger entered me and I wailed with pleasure and despair. The wave of my orgasm was building; I could feel it deep within my core.

"You're safe with me, always," he whispered.

I broke with those words, their truth ringing down my resistance like an earthquake. I begged him over and over to let me come, tears skating my cheeks in relief when he said, "That's my girl. Come for me."

Release tore through me, pulling against my muscles and turning my mental barricades to dust.

As he undid my restraints and carried me to bed, I'd never felt more exposed, loved.

I'd never felt so strong.

# UNFOLDING

## K D Grace

Lena sprawled on the carpet in front of the fireplace with Simon practically on top of her. He had opened her blouse and coaxed both of her tits to play peekaboo above the lacy sweep of her balconette bra. Her nipples were slicked with his warm saliva, standing at full attention, as he alternately thumbed and licked and sucked. His hard-on threatened the integrity of his jeans as she stroked and kneaded his crotch.

Her panties were way past damp, and the shift and press of her puss against the gusset made her well aware of her own heavy swell. She'd already let things go too far, and as his hand slipped beneath her skirt, insinuating itself up and over the inside of her thigh, she knew if she waited much longer it would be too late. With an effort that took all the willpower she could muster, she pushed him away and went for his fly. He protested with a muffled, "Mmmph," against her left nipple.

"I want your cock in my mouth," she lied. Okay, it wasn't exactly a lie. She just didn't want his cock in her mouth right now, but it was self-preservation that mattered at this point, she reminded herself.

"Not yet." He surprised her by pushing her hand away from his fly and raising her fingers to the hot press of his lips. "I want to feel you." He held her gaze, face barely above the horizon of her breasts. "All of you." The hand under her skirt homed in on the elastic of her panties, wriggling like a rabbit slipping under a fence.

She tried to squirm away, but he'd caught her completely off guard. She'd never had her offer of a blow job turned down before or even slightly delayed. She knew with a knotting in her stomach that there was no turning back. His weight was mostly on her, and he was stealthy, god yes! He was so stealthy. Before she could even think of a Plan B, his hand was already in, stroking her closely trimmed muff like it was his favorite pet.

"Please don't," she gasped. "Please don't do thaaa—" Her words ended in a gasp as his thumb raked her clit so skillfully that she sucked air and her pussy soaked itself anew in appreciation. She struggled to find her voice again. "I have...I don't want...I have very large..." She squirmed and bucked, digging her heels into the carpet, trying to push herself away, but her efforts had the opposite effect, raising her secret right into his hand. He stroked, and she gasped. In spite of the rush of heat to her face, her pussy griped and trembled in tight, underground wavelets.

"Oh, my god," he half whispered. Suddenly he was shoving at her skirt and tugging at her panties with both hands. She stopped fighting and felt tears threatening her eyes. This wasn't supposed to happen. Didn't she know to be more cautious? Hadn't she carefully trained herself? But now it was too late. Simon was too strong.

By the time she got around to half sobbing, "I'm sorry, I'm so sorry," he had completely shoved her skirt aside and dragged off her panties. He pressed her legs wide apart with rough palms, breathing like a cyclone in hot blasts against her splayed pussy.

"Jesus, woman, what on earth are you sorry about? I've never seen anything like it."

At first she thought he was teasing her, making fun of her, but then his thick fingers raked upward from her perineum to where her lips folded around her cunt-hole. The words he spoke practically trembled up his throat. "My god, they're exquisite. They're like wings, deep red bird wings folded over your pussy, protecting you, hiding you."

"Wha—?"

"Let me see, Lena. Please let me see." He slid his heavy middle finger upward and inward, then turned it, and she felt herself unfolding, opening like the rise of the curtains at the beginning of a play.

"But I'm so big," she half whispered, half apologized.

"I can see that." His breath moved over her swollen land-scape, making her humid and sticky. "Dear lord in heaven, I can see that. I've never seen such lovely, heavy, abundant lips."

"But I thought—"

"Sh! Just lie still for me and let me enjoy." He cupped her butt in his hands and pulled her close to his face, close enough that his breath blew down her cleft in warm little gusts. His hands were big enough that he spread her heavy labia with his thumbs and worried them wide open as he lapped his way up the valley between. Then, with a blissed-out sigh, he took each of her lips in his mouth in turn, tongued them, fondled them, nibbled them until she ground and arched and writhed, until she felt heavy as lead, and so thick that any minute the very swell of her might force her legs wide apart and split her in two. She wondered how he even had room for her hugeness in his mouth. But he ate at her ravenously, like she was ripe fruit, the tropical kind, the kind that grows in the humid heat, deep red and bursting with juices. His tongue and teeth released those juices, and he slurped them, suckled them, drank them until there was no stopping the explosion that burst from between, rippling and convulsing up over them.

Then she heard him grunt as though he'd just been gut punched. He whispered a curse, and his grip became nearly painful before he caught his breath and slid up next to her, his face shining with her ripeness. He offered her a sheepish smile as he pulled her to his still-heaving chest, nearly smothering her in his embrace. "Lena, I came in my pants."

"What?" She tried to pull away.

But he held her tight, and offered an embarrassed chuckle. "Sorry. This has never happened before. I'm the king of delayed gratification, trust me. I just wasn't prepared for how exquisite you look down there. It was like a religious experience, it was like—"

"Stop it, please," she interrupted him. "I can't think."

He pressed a pussy-flavored kiss to her lips and continued. "Lena, some men are tit men, some men are ass men. Me, I'm a labia man. I completely and totally adore labia. I have since the first time I figured out that the differences between girls and guys were a good thing, back when I was a kid, back when I played 'I'll show you mine if you show me yours' with Marcy Fischer next door. And porn? Well, it just doesn't do it for me unless the woman's lips dangle and pout. There's just something about those lovely, heavy lady lips that makes me stiff. And yours, well, your lady lips are the most beautiful I've ever seen. Honest."

"The girls in gym class used to call me 'Flapper' when I was in school." Even now it made her blush, and her gut clenched at the thought.

"They were probably just jealous. Probably didn't have any real flaps of their own," Simon said, and she couldn't keep from chuckling.

Simon had cleaned himself as best he could in her bathroom, and they now sat snuggled together on the sofa, sipping the wine he'd brought that night. His hand was already resting expectantly on her upper thigh.

Suddenly she was serious again. "I thought about...you know, having surgery, making them smaller."

"Fuck that!" He gulped a harsh breath and paled. "That would be like erasing the Mona Lisa's smile."

"Oh, don't worry, I decided not to." She shook her head hard to reassure him. "I couldn't. They're just so, so..."

"So what?" His hand had begun to knead and caress and make tight little circles higher and higher on her thigh.

She shifted beneath his caresses, almost without thinking adjusting her perch on the sofa to ease his efforts. "They're just so sensitive. They're... Well, I think they're at least as sensitive as my clit. She glanced into his eyes, blushed hard, then focused her attention back on his relentless hand. "You have no idea how good it feels, even the touch of my panties down there. But..."

His breathing had accelerated again, and his cock strained the denim. "Tell me."

She shifted and leaned into him, suddenly anxious to talk to someone about what had been her secret pleasure and shame for all these years, someone who seemed to understand. "The rub of the panties, that's just the start. I often don't wear them because, well it's more comfortable for me without them, less... distracting." She nodded down to her crotch. "You saw how big my lips are. Even when they're not aroused, which they almost always are, I have to be careful how I sit down."

"Does it hurt?" He breathed.

"No! It doesn't hurt. It feels good. It feels so damn good that I—"

"That you need to go masturbate." His cock jerked like an animal trying to escape, and for a second, she wondered if he'd jizzed himself again.

When she was sure he had managed containment, she continued. "Oh, I don't need to masturbate."

He was wide-eyed, pupils dilated. His voice had gone suddenly throaty. "You don't?"

She shook her head. "No. I just come." She tried to sound matter-of-fact about it lest her enthusiasm send his cock over the edge again.

"Unbelievable."

"I don't let anyone see me down there." She spoke softly now. "I didn't mean to let you see."

"So what do you do then?" He asked. "I mean surely if someone tried to push into you they'd notice, whether you let them see or not."

She shifted closer to his warmth. "I give great blow jobs. Most guys don't care to look any farther once they've come. Just to be sure I tell them giving blow jobs makes me come, too. That usually takes care of any obligation they might feel for further exploration."

He leaned forward and placed a gentle brush of a kiss against her mouth and pushed a lock of stray hair behind her ear. "But eventually, maybe not the first time, but eventually, they must want to come inside you."

"There is no eventually." She fought the unexpected lump in her throat. "I can't risk it."

"A shame," he said, holding her gaze with sad eyes. "All that exquisite beauty unappreciated. It's a damn shame. Was I intended to be a one-night stand, too?"

She lifted her hand to stroke his sun-bleached hair. "I think we're way past what I intended by now, Simon."

He kissed her again, this time with plenty of skillful tongue, and his stroking of her thigh now deliberately scrunched skirt between tense fingers. "I won't be distracted by a blow job, Lena, not when I know what you've got down there. And now that I do know," he eyed her expectantly. "I promise I won't humiliate myself again."

She held his gaze for a long moment, struggling with the last remnants of doubt before she released a shaky sigh and gave him an almost imperceptible nod of her head.

His breath quivered through him like she had offered him the cure for his affliction. He shoved her skirt out of the way to discover her cunt was bare.

She offered an embarrassed smile. "After...what happened, well, I'm just too swollen and uncomfortable for panties."

"I can see that," he gasped as she opened her legs for her unfurling. Without warning, he dropped onto the floor between her spread thighs, and for a long moment, he said nothing. He seemed to be mesmerized by the sight of her lips plumped like they were ready to pillow a cock seeking the decadent comfort of her slickened hole. Her lips were always at the ready, but never like this; never had she allowed them to make a man stiff, never had she allowed them to make a man want. The very thought made her slippery and engorged with want of her own.

When his eyes had had their feast, his hands took over, stroking the insides of her labia with his thumbs while cradling the outside against the crook of his index fingers, stroking and stretching and tugging, every caress making her feel even heavier. His face was only inches away, and his breath bathed the splay of her in thick, tetchy heat.

She was teetering on the edge when he pulled away and looked up at her, face once more dewed in her juices. "The view down here makes me incredibly hard, and I'd like to salvage my reputation now, if that's okay with you." He nodded down to his overworked fly. "I'm not insubstantial." He offered her a tight smile. "Might do you some good."

"It might, at that," she breathed. The clench in her chest matched the one between her legs as she watched him wriggle free of his jeans. As his cock poked its helmeted head over the waistband of his boxers, she happily agreed that he was not at all insubstantial. With unsteady efforts, she positioned her bare feet on the sofa and lifted her ass to give him a better view. The thought of her lewd display made her heavier still. She had never let anyone deliberately, blatantly, lustfully gaze at her cunt, winged for flight as it was, with her heavy, dangly, ripe-fruit lips open wide for the embrace. And now, not only were her bits being gazed upon and adored, they were being made love to.

As Simon rose to position himself, his cock brushed against her labia and she jerked and tensed. "Sh, sh!" He pressed a kiss against her mouth. "Don't be nervous. Just relax and let me get us there. Together this time." Then, with a soft grunt, he pushed into her.

She'd had fantasies about how it would be when she finally trusted a man enough to let him slide in between her swell. In her fantasies, it was always gentle, easy, lingering. She couldn't have been more wrong. It was as though someone had turned rutting wild animals loose in the house. The incredible friction of having something so substantial inside her, something that didn't run off batteries, something that had a mind of its own, drove her to mad thrusting and humping. She wrapped her legs around him and dug her heels in for the ride. He cupped her buttocks in his hands and pulled her tighter to him. She wasn't sure if it was just the natural way Simon fucked or if he had somehow intuited what would offer her enormous labia the most pleasure. Either way, he got the job done exquisitely. He undulated, almost circled, with his hips each time he thrust, so that his cock caressed and stroked her engorged lips. And each time he thrust and caressed her lips, they tightened their embrace around him.

"Oh, my god, Lena," he gasped. "I can't hold it any longer. I'm sorry, but I have to come." But it didn't matter. He had nothing to apologize for. As his cock spasmed inside her, she arched up like her back would break and howled the mother of all orgasms into the world. It began as tremors and quakes around Simon's jerking cock. Then it gathered momentum and erupted outward like wildfire up her spine, over her belly and breasts, shooting straight through the crown of her head. There, it exploded into wave after wave of pure, superheated lust that collapsed in on itself back down to her open-winged cunt, fluttering and trembling tight around Simon's thick pulsations.

They dozed together on the sofa, and when she woke it was to the feel of his fingers tugging and pulling on her distended pussy lips. She was still swollen tight around his cock, which didn't seem any more flaccid than it had been when he put it inside her. Once he realized she was awake, he offered her a lingering kiss with a lazy tongue circling and stroking the inside of her mouth. "I want to bathe you down there," he said when he pulled away enough to catch his breath. Before she could protest, he added, "I want to tend to you, admire you, take care of those luscious pussy lips. It'll be good. I promise."

After she'd shown him the bath gels and candles and other pampering goodies, he shooed her out and she left him to prepare the bath. His cock was still at full attention when he came for her. She was wrapped in a soft chenille robe, but he was still completely naked. He led her into the steamy confines of the bathroom, which smelled of lavender and geranium. A tub filled with white froth beckoned. When she reached for her sash, he eased her hand away, knelt in front of her and from a position that felt like nothing less than one of obeisance, he loosened her robe and opened it. He ran the flat of his hands over her belly, then around to caress her bottom. His breath raised a goose-fleshed path below her navel as he pressed a humid kiss against her tight curls. It was then that she noticed he had found her razor and placed it at the ready on the side of the tub.

He smiled up at her from where he knelt, then ran his hand over her muff. "Do you mind? I love pubic curls, I adore women with bushes, but in your case"—he eased her thighs apart slightly, and her lips pushed their way front and center against the stroke of his fingers—"there should be no distractions. You should be smooth and bare and huge and totally on display."

How could she argue with that? Hadn't he embraced her secret with pleasure, even adoration? Suddenly she could think of nothing she'd like better than a totally bare puss to showcase her outrageous lips. Before he steered her toward the bathtub, he opened her legs just enough to insinuate his mouth into the space between so he could suck and tug her labia like a nursing colt. Then, just when she was ready to collapse against him and forsake bathing for fucking, he pulled away, helped her out of her robe, and guided her to sit on the edge of the tub, leaning back against the cool, steamy tiles.

He stepped naked into the froth and once again knelt before her. Then he eased her legs apart. She heard the hitch of his breath as she shifted her hips and spread her thighs farther for easy access. She offered a soft, throaty chuckle that echoed wet and horny off the bathroom walls. "Are you sure your hands are steady enough for this?"

"It'll be a piece of cake," he said. "You're already well trimmed."

He commenced his efforts, lathering and soaping and sculpting until she ground her ass against the tiles at the delicious sensations his ministering created below her mons.

"Hold still," he commanded, as he took up the razor. Though it wasn't necessary, he slipped three fingers of his left hand into the valley between her lips to rest against her grasping hole, to steady her. He worried his bottom lip deliciously with his teeth as he carefully but confidently scraped the razor along the outer edge of her muff. He rinsed and inspected his work, then repeated his efforts.

By the time he was attending to the last scrapings, her clit was standing at full attention from beneath its hood. Her lips had distended to a full caress of his fingers, and he was breathing like he'd been digging ditches rather than shaving pussy. That finished, he lay the razor aside and rained a heavy drizzle of water from a thick bath sponge down over her clean-shaven mound. He inspected it for smoothness with his lips, then with a darting flick of his tongue, which migrated farther south to slide over her clit and offer just enough pressure to make her jump.

"There," he whispered. "Now there are no distractions, all paths lead to your delicious, pendulous, riotous pout, which I will pay homage to."

This time, he held her distended labia wide and drizzled water from the sponge down the valley between, and she ground her ass and moaned. He lifted her right foot from the tub and nibbled her toes and lapped water off her instep and ankle before he brought it to rest on his shoulder, splaying her ripe, verdant landscape still wider, still closer to his hungry eyes. He sluiced another sponge full of warm, fragrant water down her valley and all the way back over her gripping anus.

It made her gush with warm sticky girlie juices, juices she could imagine pearling just at the bottom of the place where her hole opened and gaped for his cock. And his cock, my god, his cock looked big enough to split her in two, rising of its own volition engorged and salient amid the diminishing foam.

"It's yoni in Sanskrit, your pussy is," he said, lowering his face to press a kiss on each fully spread lip. "It's the temple, the sacred space, the source of all that exists. I knew these things instinctively. I didn't have to read them, because I worshipped at the sacred temple long before I knew why it had such power over me." This time the kisses were tight tugs with little nips of his teeth, like he was daintily nibbling on a choice morsel. "And your sacred temple is so exquisitely adorned, so completely inviting." He now lifted her other leg onto his shoulder, nestled her down tight against his mouth then entered her temple face-first, lapping her path with long sinuous passes of his tongue, as though it were the acolyte, preparing the way for the high priest. She flooded his face, shifting and writhing and spreading her slickness, practically causing a tidal wave as she bucked against his nibblings.

"If you could see what I see," he breathed. "You're heavy and swollen like you could contain the whole universe. And the dark, warm hole at the center of you draws and pulls and drags everything to it. I'm powerless in your pull, I'm yours to command."

"Then fuck me," she rasped, grabbing his hair and curling her fingers skull deep. "The temple has been empty for too damn long."

With one more tight kiss against her labia, which now felt

bigger than the whole room, and more wet and steamy, he cupped her bottom and positioned her. His eyes fluttered, his breath caught as he settled her onto his cock one slow, deliciously, torturous inch at a time. The heavy velvet curtains of her labia parted for him, swallowed him down, allowing him entrance into the holy of holies. Then he began the long, silky wet slide into her hole, into the depths of her temple. She shuddered all over at the feeling of fullness—her fullness pressed so tightly against his own. Water swirled and danced around them, rising up from under the bubbles that had now all but gone. Her nipples pearled hard against his chest as he held her to him, thrusting up into her with his circular, cunt-deep undulations. Undulations became poundings and the swirl and dance of the water became a tempest breaking in waves over the edge of the tub onto the floor. And when they both came, the bathroom walls echoed with their cries and moans of pleasure.

He helped her out of the tub and gently toweled her dry, kneeling to linger over her newly shaven pussy. Then she took him by the hand and led him to her bed. As he snuggled in next to her, he nestled his fingers in between her legs and lovingly tugged and caressed her still-heavy lips. "At last," he whispered, "Venus is risen on her half shell, and she is wondrous, indeed."

# MARRIED

## Abigail Grey

In her sweatpants and beat-up tank top, Jane flipped through her Netflix queue. Sighing at the severe lack of good movies to watch instantly, she turned her attention to her laptop. Tightening her ponytail holder and straightening her glasses, she got down to the after-hours job of grading papers and folding laundry while catching up on her guilty pleasure cop comedy series.

In the middle of typing another mind-numbingly boring response email to yet another overly concerned parent, a chat box popped up in her window.

*Hey. Haven't seen you around here lately.*

Jane sat back, a semi-hysterical laugh coming to her lips. She hadn't seen a message from this account in years. She looked behind her, into the kitchen, craning her neck to peer down the hallway where her kids were sleeping. "Honey?" she called out.

From down the hallway, she heard his answering yell. "Yeah, sweetheart?"

She shook her head, eyes glued to the screen and the surprising instant message. "Nothing. Never mind." She closed it out with another chuckle, continuing the email she was writing.

Moments later, it popped up again. *What are you doing?*

She rolled her eyes before responding. *Grading papers.*

*Oh yeah,* she read in his response a few minutes later. *You're a teacher or something, right?*

Jane decided to play along and see where this specter from her past would lead her. *Yup, second grade.*

*Sounds like a barrel of laughs. Care for a distraction?*

Jane laughed with a lightning-quick response. *Absolutely not. I have way too much to do. I mean, these Arctic animals may just wander off. Or, you know, one of the uber-anal super moms might freak out if she doesn't have the winter project—that she spent all night on—graded and back in her hands the next day.* Jane knew his distractions would be more than she could handle while continuing her nightly routine of multitasking work, housework and her small amount of daily "me" time.

*Oh, fuck those super moms. They'll live. Come on. What are you wearing?*

Looking down at her ratty sleep clothes, Jane sighed. *Nothing interesting.*

*What, nothing fun to get your husband all hot for you after grading papers?*

She could imagine his smirk as he typed it. She typed back, *Nah, he's working on some reports for work or something.*

*You're no fun. Make it up for me. What would you be wearing if I was there right now?*

Jane thought back. What would she wear for this man, the builder of some of her best nights in college? *Okay, okay. How about a satin set, shorts and this little tank top? A little lace, all silky and smooth?*

*That sounds nice. Do you like that set of pajamas?*

Jane set her things aside and lay back with her laptop, clicking a pen on her knee. *Yeah, they're really nice. And I love the way they feel on my skin.*

*Tell me how they feel.*

*I especially like them after I've taken a really long bath, after I've just shaved my legs smooth. Feeling the satin slide over my smooth skin is so decadent.*

*It's not just on your legs it feels smooth, is it?*

Jane smiled a little. *You remembered.*

*Of course. It's not often a girl tells me how good it feels to get fucked right after she shaves her pussy.*

*I had forgotten about that. Those pajamas feel amazing after that, too.*

*That's really too bad.*

*What are you talking about? Why would that be bad?*

*I would hate to rip your favorite pair of pajamas when I got there.*

Jane dropped her pen. She felt the flush creep up her cheeks. *Rip them? Why would you do that?*

*To get to that luscious pair of tits you used to send me pictures of ages ago. I can still imagine having them right here in front of me.*

Jane laughed quietly. Both the bane and pride of her body, the naturally large breasts she'd been blessed with had served Jane well in the past. *Oh, well, that makes some sense. But what if I didn't want you to rip them?*

*That's an easy one. You'd have to be tied down.* Jane sighed and snuggled into the cushion at that comment, continuing to read his message as her body continued to heat up. *Now that I've said it, I really feel like tearing those satin pajamas to shreds.*

*So with my hands tied to the headboard, satin strings*

*hanging from around my arms and hips... You realize, I'm sure, by that point I'd be begging for your hands somewhere,* Jane typed out.

*Oh, of course. And I would indulge you, in a way. Perhaps I would start with a hand winding around your neck, squeezing a little. Run it down your arm, over your body, until I can grip your hip and grind my cock into you.*

Jane squirmed on the couch. *That would definitely start me begging. It's been too long since I've felt the rub of a hard cock.*

*Hubby isn't keeping you satisfied?*

Jane sat back for a moment before responding. It had been quite a while since Adam, her husband, had even brought it up. So often lately, he was working in his office for hours, even after she went to bed. *You know what they say about married life. All work, no play. We don't have time between our jobs, the kids, random family schedule stuff.*

*Too bad. An ass like yours needs to be used, hard and often. Know what I'm picturing right now?*

*No, but I think I could guess.* Jane took a breath in and smiled. *I'm guessing you're thinking of the picture I sent you when I was on all fours, the one where you can see my ass really well?*

*Not exactly.*

Jane waited, nearly holding her breath in anticipation. The creativity of his mind had gotten her through some horrible all-nighters in college. She remembered nights that she had been so tempted to call him, to hear if the voice behind the ideas could inspire as well. He had seemed to have an automatic insight to her need, whether she needed a gentle hand, a heavier one, or even one wielding rope and one a bucket of ice. And the anonymity of the medium, messaging and emailing, had opened her own coffers of fantasy. He knew things about her that she was still ashamed she had opened up about.

*What I'm thinking is you, tied by your wrists to the head-board like before, but flipped over onto your knees. Your cheek is on your pillow, your tits brushing the bed and your ass up in the air.*

Jane shivered, closing her eyes to savor the image. She could see it clearly in her mind: the pillows haphazard on the bed, the sheets and blankets tangled at the foot and around one of her legs. She could imagine feeling that presence behind her right before his hand curved up her ass and around her waist. The bed would dip as his weight settled behind her. She would squeal as his cock parted her wet pussy lips.

Her chat box lit up with his new message in the middle of her little fantasy. *What I really wish I could feel is your tight little ass wrapped around my cock.*

Jane amended the image in her head as she typed back, *You know, the last time I did that with my husband, it hurt, and not in a good way.*

*Oh, babe, I could definitely make up for that. We could get you all kinds of hot and just go nice and easy. Can you think about that for me? Think about my cock splitting your ass, so slowly. You'd feel that burn, but it would go away so fast. Can you picture it? Feel it?*

*Yes, I can think about it. I remember how it feels.*

*How does it feel? Tell me. Tell me what it feels like to have a big cock stretching out your ass.*

*It feels good. I just feel so full when I get fucked that way. And it feels so dirty, so wrong. I love how wrong it feels some-times.*

*That's right, you like being a dirty little slut, don't you? Getting your ass fucked hard by some guy who will just take what he wants?*

Jane's mind reeled and her hand crept between her legs. A quick rub over the seam of her sweatpants reminded her of how it felt when he turned her on. She could tell she was getting wet and swollen just thinking about his words.

*I remember something else that makes you feel full. Do you remember?*

Jane's mind flipped through so many scenarios. She had told him about her gang-bang fantasy, her fantasy about her kitchen utensils, the one in the shower; which one did he mean?

His message brought it back. *Do you remember my fist?*

Jane felt her abdomen clench. *Yes, I remember.*

*Did you ever do it? Did you ever take a whole fist since we've talked? Felt your little pussy stretch so much, wanting to scream it out, fighting against how much it hurts?*

Jane's eyes went wide. Her breathing got shallower and faster. Fingers shaking, she typed out her answer.

*Not yet.*

A sudden flurry of activity from her husband's office at the end of the hall made Jane look up. Adam stood in the doorway, wearing the old T-shirt from their alma mater. His hair was mussed, like he'd been running his fingers through it. Jane zoomed in on his hands, the ones that had held her down, tied her up and tormented her since the day she gave in to his online suggestions. The creative inspiration in his typing definitely showed through in the other ways he used his hands on her. As she watched, he clenched one into a fist, his wedding band glinting on his finger.

"Bedroom?" he asked her.

She grinned, determined to make time tonight. "Bedroom," she confirmed.

# COOK'S TREAT

## Elizabeth Coldwell

Rich chocolate buttercream. Are there three nicer words in the English language? Well, okay, maybe the ones Mark whispers when we're lying tangled in the sheets together, his fingers tracing idle figure eights on my bare hip, but those are pretty close.

Curling up in bed with my husband would have been the perfect way to spend this rainy Saturday afternoon, but he's still caught up in the backup caused by a crash on the motorway, on his way home from some dull business conference in Manchester. Baking his favorite cupcakes will let him know how much I've missed him and helps to pass the time while I wait for his return.

There's something incredibly soothing about measuring and sifting and beating, while heavy raindrops beat against the windows. It helps me to forget the outside world can be an unpredictable place of heavy storms and traffic accidents when the kitchen is so cozy, the air warm and smelling of vanilla.

A dozen cakes stand cooling in their floral paper cases on a wire rack, mouthwateringly tempting even without their thick crown of frosting. Humming along to the tune playing on the radio, I cream together butter and sugar until the mixture turns fluffy and pale and my wrist feels the first, strangely rewarding twinges of pain. Some TV chef once claimed that baking is all about precise chemical reactions, and that's why you shouldn't try to alter the recipe. Too much flour, too little baking powder, and your sponge mixture will fail to rise.

I must really have sex on my mind, because I can't help thinking of that as a chemical reaction, too: hormones blending in a rich mixture of need and desire to create the most scrumptious results. Even after all these years, I'm proud to say I still know exactly how to get Mark's passion rising. Though that's not to say our bedroom recipes don't need a little variation from time to time. You wouldn't want to eat cake that's old and dry, so why should you let your sex life go stale, either?

Turning my attention back to my baking, I beat in a level tablespoon of cocoa powder, a few drops of vanilla extract, and my frosting is complete. Piped in careful swirls on top of each cake, decorated with a scattering of chocolate sprinkles and silvered sugar balls, it makes the perfect finishing touch. Already, I'm looking forward to the moment when my teeth sink through the rich topping to the soft, moist sponge beneath. Hard as it may be, I'm saving that pleasure 'til Mark's home, but that doesn't mean I can't eat the last remnants of frosting from the bowl while I wait, just like I used to when I was a kid. Cook's treat.

Reaching out, I scoop up a dollop with my finger. Eyes closed, I'm licking off the sweet mixture, sighing with relish like a porn star lapping the last drops of come off her costar's cock, when an amused voice says, "Now, there's a sight for sore eyes."

"Mark!" There's a guilty tone to my voice, almost as though he's caught me cheating on him, down on my knees on the kitchen floor with another man's dick in my mouth. But underneath my surprise, I'm just glad to have him safely back in the warmth of the kitchen.

Even the short journey from the car to the front door has dampened the shoulders of his jacket and his hair with glistening droplets among the salt-and-pepper curls. My heart can't help but beat a little faster at the sight of him, a matching pulse between my legs reinforcing the pang of lust I feel. Mark might have been my husband for nearly a decade, but there are times, like now, when being with him is like the first time all over again.

His gaze flicks from me to the cupcake-laden table and back. "Looks like you've been busy in my absence."

"Well, I thought that seeing as you'd been stuck in that jam for ages a nice, gooey cake and a cup of tea might cheer you up."

He grins, pulling me into his arms. "Oh, it will. But first, I'd like to try some of that frosting...."

Just as I did, he dips his finger into the mixing bowl. But when he draws out some of the frosting, he doesn't immediately lick it off. Instead, he daubs it onto the end of my nose before bending his head to softly kiss it away. "Mmm, gorgeous," he murmurs, making it clear he's referring to me as much as the chocolate icing. "And I've got to have more...."

In my bare feet, I have to stretch up to kiss him properly, feeling just a hint of stubble as our faces touch. Mark's skin carries the vaguest scent of the car interior, warm plastic and pine-scented air freshener, the legacy of being cooped up inside it for so long. His tongue slides between my lips, staking claim to my mouth. Liquid heat rushes through me, my body coming alive at my husband's touch. My fingers curl in his wet hair as he pushes me back against the wall. It never grows old, never gets stale, this feeling of being in his arms, loved and wanted. But Mark has more than just kissing in mind. His hands burrow under the hem of my top, warm against my bare flesh. Pressing against his crotch, I feel the hardness of him through his jeans, impossible to ignore, and wonder if he's been thinking about me on his long, boring journey, distracting himself from the queue of unmoving traffic ahead of him with fantasies of what he'd do to me once he got home.

Whatever those fantasies involved, I'm fairly sure it wasn't the bowl that sits on the kitchen table, bearing the remains of my chocolate frosting. It's given him ideas, though.

"Strip for me, Lynda," he purrs in my ear. "Let me take a good long look at my little domestic goddess."

I love it when he gives me orders. Mark doesn't often take control, but when he does, the results always have my pussy flowing like a river in full spate. Just being told to strip has me soaking my panties as I hurry to obey.

My black chef's apron hits the floor, followed by the rest of my clothes. Mark says nothing, just stands there watching me with a smile of pure appreciation threatening to split his face in two. After all this time, it always feels good to be reminded that he doesn't get bored with looking at me.

His next move is a simple one. The zip of his fly comes down, and his cock is out, just like that. Long and fat, with the head already poking free from its sheath of velvety skin. It looks good enough to eat—which, I quickly realize, is Mark's intention.

Dipping his fingers in the bowl, he brings them out covered in frosting. Smearing the rich brown goo along his shaft, he doesn't need to give any further instruction. Without being told, I sink to the floor so I can take that beautiful thing in my mouth.

His posture is one of pure dominance, hands on his hips as he looks down at me, and I feel delightfully submissive as I begin to lick every last scrap of frosting from his hot, salty skin. Frosted cock; who'd have believed how tasty it could be?

Soon, my ministrations have gone beyond the simple task of cleaning him. My hand cups Mark's balls, gently rolling the taut spheres together, and he sighs his approval. My head bobs more vigorously as I swallow his length, taking as much as I can into the wet vacuum of my throat.

"Mmm, I love the way you suck me."

Something in Mark's supremely relaxed tone makes me long to take him out of his comfort zone. There's just a little frosting left in the bowl, and almost before he's aware of what I'm doing, I've broken off from sucking him to retrieve it. My finger paints the stuff down the seam of my husband's balls, all the way to the dark pucker of his ass. Misplaced squeamishness means I've been loath to lick him there in the past, but now my tongue laps up the trail of frosting, stimulating him in places I've never explored before. When the wet tip swipes over the entrance to his ass, I swear his knees buckle.

"Fuck, Lynda, that's amazing. But I want to come in your pussy, not your mouth."

With that, he hoists me up and sets me down on the table's edge, well away from the litter of utensils I used in my baking. Letting his jeans drop to the floor, Mark moves between my splayed thighs. Throwing an arm around his neck, I feel him slide his cock into me in one smooth, assured thrust. It may still be raining outside, but that doesn't seem to matter anymore. Outside could be a million miles away, now that my husband is here with me. I'm totally wrapped up in the feeling of him pumping in and out of me, deep and slow. My bottom scoots along the scrubbed pine tabletop, Mark's big hands gripping handfuls of my soft, round cheeks to pull me back toward him. Every thrust takes me a little closer to the point where my body seems to dissolve in on itself, aided by the steady circling of my own middle finger on my clit.

Sweeter than frosting, more decadent than the finest chocolate, my orgasm cries out to be savored. Mark's climax follows hot after my own, filling me with his thick cream. It's a recipe for perfect satisfaction.

"I love you so much," I sigh, resting my head on Mark's shoulder. "And you may kiss the cook."

He does, pressing his lips to the top of my head as I nestle into his embrace, thinking again just how lucky I am to be with him.

"So," he says, when we finally break apart, "I believe you were saying something about a cup of tea and one of those very tasty-looking cupcakes?"

"That's right."

"Well...why don't we take them to bed, enjoy them there?" he asks, thumb stroking my pebbled nipple. His smile is one of pure erotic intent, and I know I'm about to sample my very special cook's treat all over again.

# HOLLYWOOD ROMANCE

## Veronica Wilde

The Starlite Movie Cinema loomed above Claudia in the summer afternoon sunlight. She hadn't been inside since she'd graduated from high school nine years ago, although it was a favorite teenage memory of hers. The Starlite was an old-style movie theater, the kind with an actual stage, velvet curtains and just one screen: a landmark of nostalgia and lost dreams slowly decaying on Main Street in her hometown. No doubt it was unable to compete with modern multiplexes but she was still surprised and sad to hear, while visiting her parents, that it would be torn down in late August. Right away she knew she had to pay the old movie theater a final visit. Living two hours away in Chicago, she didn't visit her home-town that often and the lot would probably be a pile of dust the next time she was here.

As she stood on the sidewalk now, the building looked decrepit and ratty in the summer sunlight. The unlit marquee sign was blank and so were the glass poster cases for coming attractions.

Claudia pulled tentatively at one of the heavy double doors, expecting it to be locked. To her surprise, it opened easily.

In the cool, dim foyer, movie stars such as Humphrey Bogart and Marilyn Monroe stared down at her with painted eyes from the walls. The cashier booth was dark, too; she pushed through the next set of doors to find herself in front of an empty concession stand. On either side of the lobby, enormous green-carpeted staircases waited beckoningly. She knew the left one led up to the men's restroom and the right one led up to the women's—but more importantly, they both led to the Starlite's forbidden balcony.

A smile of blissful memory curved Claudia's lips. The balcony. Never had any place done so much to inspire her sexual fantasies. When she was in high school, everyone whispered about who had done what to whom up there. Officially the balcony was forbidden to the public due to some kind of fire-hazard regulation, and it had been blocked off with velvet ropes for as long as she could remember. Every showing, the movie-theater manager would come through with a flashlight to make sure it was empty. But all of that simply made the balcony an erotic dare that everyone wanted to try.

Claudia got the chance herself one night with her first boyfriend. They headed up the opposite staircases two minutes apart to avoid the suspicion of the concession clerks. Slipping under the velvet rope, Claudia's heart pounded as she entered the waiting darkness. Twelve rows of seats faced the screen. The movie looked bigger and better from up here, but she forgot all that as her boyfriend took her by the waist and kissed her.

Then the screen turned bright, exposing the rest of the balcony, and Claudia saw a young woman four rows up. Her sweater and bra were pushed up to expose her firm breasts while her boyfriend's hand worked between her spread legs. Claudia couldn't stop staring. It was the first time she'd ever seen a woman exhibit herself so brazenly in public, and it was the first time she realized how exciting that might feel. Although Claudia never dared to go quite that far herself in the balcony on that night or any other, her fantasies began to stray into uncharted territory. Dreams of riding a hard-bodied man in one of those balcony chairs, or being groped by a stranger who stayed faceless in the dark, haunted her sexual thoughts through college and beyond.

"If only," she said to herself now with a sigh.

She walked into the theater, shivering a little in her thin summer dress. Before her stretched hundreds of empty seats, all facing an enormous dark screen. The same dusty-looking velvet curtains waited on each side of the stage. Her heart gave a little pang. Why did people prefer boring multiplexes when they could watch movies in a place with romance and ambience?

A sudden clicking echoed through the theater. She gasped as a rattle followed and then, to her astonishment, the screen lit up. A scratchy black-and-white movie began to play, the credits announcing David Selznick as producer.

"This can't be happening," she whispered. She looked around for someone, anyone, but the theater was empty. Feeling spooked, she hurried back into the lobby.

A man was coming down the stairs. A young man, with dark hair falling in his eyes and tattoos on his hard-muscled arms. She stepped back against the concession stand, startled, and he looked up and went still.

Neither of them moved. There was something familiar about this guy, something she recognized in his almond-shaped dark eyes. A wordless memory stirred inside her. But she couldn't say what it was.

"Claudia," he said. "Claudia Charbonneau. Right?"

He didn't take his eyes from her as he reached the lobby. She stared harder at him, trying to define the tumultuous emotion rising inside her. Where had they met before? The logical answer was high school, but she'd had a small graduating class—and he was way too cute to not remember.

A faint smile played across his lips as he walked toward her. Tall and lean, with rumpled black hair, in his gray T-shirt and jeans, he definitely didn't look like anyone who had gone to her preppy high school.

"You don't remember me," he said. "I'm Levi Schroeder."

She exhaled as memory clicked into place. Levi Schroeder. *Him* she remembered very well. He'd transferred to her high school just four months before she graduated. But as the most rebellious guy in school, he'd quickly found a place in her heart—and in her fantasies. Now he was standing right in front of her, taller and more handsome than ever. His hair was cut shorter and was a uniform black, without the colored streaks that had made the teachers dislike him. His hard-muscled left bicep was inked with a new tattoo. But god help her if he didn't cause that same melting feeling inside her when he smiled.

"Right. I just didn't recognize you." She was embarrassed at how fast her heart was going. "You were a year behind me, right?"

"Yep. The new kid in town, when you were a senior."

She tucked back a strand of her long brown hair and tried to think of something witty to say. Levi had always made her nervous, but he'd made everyone nervous back then. He listened to bands none of her friends knew, had that punk hair, wore a lot of black—the standard rebel who really wasn't all that dangerous in retrospect, but at the time intimidated everyone in her sheltered small town. It didn't help that in addition to his cool and insolent style, Levi was incredibly good-looking, with a devilish smile and almond-shaped eyes so dark they looked black. Claudia had shared a study hall with him those last months of high school, but she'd never had the nerve to talk to him. Of course, Levi had been a social liability as well; he was a junior with a bad reputation, where she was a senior who wanted to date college guys.

But he looked all man to her now. She groped for the right words. "I can't believe you're, uh—" *So gorgeous, so tall, standing right in front of me,* came to mind. "Still in town," she finished. "Why are you here, anyhow? At the Starlite, I mean."

His dark brows shot up. "More like, what are you doing here? I don't even open on weekdays anymore."

"I?" Then she understood. "You *work* here?"

"I own it." Seeing her confusion, he smiled wryly. "But not for much longer. The Starlite will be torn down in two months."

"So my parents told me. Why? I love this old theater."

"You and no one else," he shrugged. "Look, I love it, too, but it's lost money every year I've owned it. I tried to make it into an indie and foreign film place, but that just doesn't sell in this small town. Even with my film school friends coming down on the weekends, I'm in the red."

"Film school… You're a filmmaker?"

Of course he was. Even back in high school, she'd known Levi Schroeder would grow up to do something creative and independent.

"Strictly indie—I'm no Spielberg. But I do need money to finance my next project and well, a major restaurant chain has offered me good money for this lot."

"That's so harsh!"

"It's so practical. There's no Hollywood romance in real life. Beautiful old buildings get torn down. Artistic films get ignored. The popular girl never dates the outcast. And so on."

He tilted his head and gave her that hypnotic smile she remembered so well.

Her face went warm. What was he referring to with that last statement? She decided to ignore it. "I'd give anything to watch another movie here."

"Then you shall." He gestured inside the theater. "Come on. *Portrait of Jennie*. It's a great old movie."

Levi ran upstairs to the projectionist's booth to restart the film while Claudia chose a seat in the middle of the theater. Sitting alone in the cool silence wasn't spooky as much as it felt...well, naughty. Her short summer dress felt too skimpy in the air-conditioned dark. *Am I really doing this?* she asked herself. *Watching an old Hollywood flick with Levi Schroeder from study hall? This is crazy.*

Levi returned with candy bars and cold bottled water. "The popcorn machines are gone, but I still keep these in the office."

She accepted a Snickers. Now that she was adjusting to his presence, she wished she had more time to ask about his current life. Specifically, she wanted to know if he had a girlfriend. Levi was talented, twenty-six and drop-dead gorgeous. No doubt many women found him as attractive as she did. Yet here he was on a hot summer afternoon, watching an old movie by himself. It was the last thing she would have expected from him in high school.

The movie began again. She found herself enjoying it, though she'd never seen many classic Hollywood black-and-white movies.

"That's Jennifer Jones," Levi explained, murmuring as if they were surrounded by an audience instead of empty seats. "She's one of my favorite actresses."

His lips so close to her ear made her shiver. "She's pretty," she managed to respond.

As the film went on, her eyes returned to Levi's thigh muscles. He was casually sprawled down in his seat, eyes on the screen, clearly wrapped up in the story. Obviously he wasn't thinking about her next to him, or imagining what it would be like to pull down the top of her dress and play with her bare breasts. Or what it would do to her if he cupped her pussy under her dress, tickling her clit until she writhed with mindless pleasure in her seat. Or, best of all, if he led her up to the balcony and bent her over the railing, then pushed up her dress and slid every inch of his cock inside her from behind.

"So?" Levi asked when the movie ended. "What did you think?"

*I think that just sitting next to you is making me dizzy.* "It was great," she managed, wishing she hadn't let herself fixate on her own fantasies during the film. Her panties were so damp they clung to her flesh.

He frowned. "You seem distracted. Old movies not your thing?"

"Oh...no, I'm just nostalgic, I guess. I have a lot of memories in this place."

"Let me guess. The balcony?"

She couldn't help blushing. "Guilty as charged. I think everyone snuck up there at some point. Despite the safety hazard."

Levi snickered. "There's no safety hazard. That was just a story to keep people out of there. I did the same thing—something about it just invites public sex. I guess some people find that a turn-on."

Her blush deepened until her cheeks were burning.

He looked closely at her and a dirty grin spread across his face. "And maybe some people still do," he said.

Claudia groped in her purse for her keys, avoiding his eyes.

"I should be going."

"Wait," he said. "I know this was supposed to be your last movie here, but if you're still in town tomorrow night, stop by. I'm hosting a private Billy Wilder double feature with *Sunset Boulevard* and *Some Like It Hot*. It's just the local arts crowd coming, no big deal."

She nodded. "I'm here all weekend."

Those mysterious black eyes were a mix of tenderness and speculation. Looking at him, she felt like she was falling into a dream. Quickly, before she said or did anything foolish, she repeated, "I should go," and quickly walked out of the Starlite into the glaring sun, where her car was waiting.

She took a deep breath. This afternoon had been like going through a time warp, an unsettling, erotic time warp. She wasn't sure what was more shocking: that she had run into Levi at all, or that he still had the ability to arouse her so powerfully.

The next night Claudia went out to dinner with her parents, then drove down to the Starlite. She was wearing a short black dress with green flowers printed on it and her sexiest black heels, an outfit that had always made her feel sexy and confident. Yet upon arrival, she found a lobby crowded with many attractive people chatting to each other as if they were at a party. The festival hadn't been advertised to the public, as far as she could tell, so apparently these were just Levi's friends. Instead of using the concession stand, they'd set up a long white-clothed table laden with pastries, crackers and cheese, and soft drinks and wine.

"Claudia." Levi pushed through the crowd. "So glad you came."

He was wearing a black shirt that emphasized his dark good looks. She tried to hide the appreciation in her eyes. "This is more like a party than any film festival I've been to."

"Unfortunately I had to lay off my employees a few months ago. Since then, I've been using the theater for festivals and themed screenings like this. Might as well while I have the space." He looked around the old lobby with obvious wistfulness in his eyes.

"You're going to miss this place when it's gone," she told him.

"More than you know. But it's time to move on. And I think Chicago will be a better place for me, socially and creatively."

Warmth flooded her entire body. He was moving to Chicago; it was almost too good to be true. She tried to keep her voice neutral as she said, "Chicago's great. There's nowhere I'd rather live."

Levi looked stunned, then happy. "I didn't know you lived there."

"Yep. I'm getting my master's in health care administration right now, but I hope to get a good local job offer when I'm done. I'd hate to move."

A clever smile crept across Levi's face.

"Well. I'd ask you to be one of my new Chicago friends this fall, but then again, you were always too good to be friends with me in high school."

"I was not!" she protested. "I didn't even know you."

"We had study hall together and you didn't talk to me once."

"You didn't talk to me, either!"

"Because you were Miss Popular, and I was the weird kid nobody liked."

"Oh, please. *Everybody* liked you. Okay, maybe 'liked' isn't the right word, but everyone thought you were so cool. You know how many girls had secret crushes on you?"

"No, I don't," he said. "Why don't you tell me how many and who?"

His black eyes danced. She could feel herself getting flustered again. Damn him. How was he able to make her so self-conscious and awkward and excited all at the same time?

"It wouldn't be a secret if I told you," she returned.

He laughed. "It's time for me to start the first movie," he said. "Why don't you pick a seat and I'll be right down."

He headed up the stairs to the projectionist's booth. Claudia watched the roll of his firm ass with a sigh.

Glancing back at the crowd, all of whom were filing into the theater, she made a decision.

She slipped up the stairs behind Levi. He had already vanished, either into the men's restroom or into an unmarked door marked OFFICE. A jolt went through her as she confronted the mysterious dark maw of the balcony. The velvet ropes from her high school days were gone, but they had been replaced by a waist-high construction barrier. Taking a deep breath, she pushed it aside and moved past it.

Twelve rows of empty seats waited before her, just like in the fantasies that had haunted her for years. Hot memories surged through her, not only of her long-ago adventures here but of the many private dreams they'd inspired. She leaned over the railing and glanced at the audience waiting below. She would just have to hope that none of them had the same idea she did.

The movie began. Quickly Claudia positioned herself in the balcony entrance and waited for him to pass. "Levi."

He stopped, his mouth dropping a little as he saw her. "Claudia—what are you doing?"

She held out a hand. "You said to pick a seat. I want to watch the movie from up here."

After a moment, his lips curved in that dirty grin she'd

seen yesterday. "If that's how you want it." He moved past the barrier, as she had, and led her to the front row.

Her heart raced as she smoothed her dress beneath her. She was actually in the Starlite's balcony—and with the cute rebel from her teenage dreams. It all seemed too incredible and erotic to be true.

Levi leaned back in his chair, stretching out his long legs. "You know you're violating management policy by being up here."

"Yes, but I'm hoping the manager realizes that this is my last chance to visit my high school memories."

"And what kind of memories were these? The manager needs to know details."

"Shush! There's a rule about not talking during the movie." She shifted in her seat, aware that her dress was hiking up her thighs.

He leaned against her and said, "In that case, you'll have to give the manager a demonstration."

The thrill of a challenge raced through Claudia. Was she really going to do this?

She was. She reached behind her and unzipped her dress, gracefully slipping out of the top. Just as casually, she unsnapped her black lace bra, tossed it aside, and settled back topless in her seat. Levi's lust-filled eyes locked on her bare breasts as she stroked her nipples to hard pink points, circling them with a light touch.

He sharply sucked in his breath. "Keep going…"

"No talking, remember?"

Claudia pulled her dress higher up her thighs, spreading her legs until Levi could see her matching black lace panties. Sliding her hand inside them, she began to rub her clit, shifting the skimpy fabric around just enough to flash him with tantalizing peeks of her pussy.

Levi gave a soft, rough growl and got on his knees. Eagerly, Claudia lifted her hips off the seat as he pulled her panties down her thighs, pushed her legs apart and began to lick her clit with exuberance and skill. A paralyzing mix of shock and bliss swept through her as his tongue bathed her entire sex in strong, agile strokes. Gasping, she pinched her own nipples, struggling not to make a sound that might alert the audience below. Levi seemed to be almost drinking from her pussy, his lips dancing over her sensitive labia until she writhed helplessly in her seat. As his talented tongue returned to her swollen clitoris, his fingers gently pushed into her tightness.

Claudia shamelessly arched her back, her hips bucking up to meet Levi's mouth in a quest for satisfaction. The combination of the darkness and the audience below ignited her blood with incandescent fever, and the sight of Levi's handsome face between her bare legs only stoked it higher. Gripping the armrests of the seat, she dropped her head back and strained her thighs wider as his tongue spiraled around her clit. Her pussy was filling with a whirlpool of warm delight, and as he rubbed another finger gently around her anus, euphoria filled her blood. Her orgasm broke inside her with an almost violent crash, a deep, liquid throbbing that flooded the seat underneath her.

She pulled away from him, embarrassed at the wet intensity of her orgasm and desperate for self-control. "Stop," she whispered. "You're making me lose my mind."

"Good."

Levi pulled her to her feet. Her legs were shaking so hard that she could barely stand on her high heels, and she leaned against him for support as she stepped out of her dress. She was totally nude now, nude in a public movie theater, and she submitted to his complete control as he led her to the wide carpeted stairs that led up to the other balcony rows. Feeling lost in a dream, she obediently stretched out on them as Levi spread her legs once more.

Yet this time he didn't touch her. Instead he rose and began to undress. She watched appreciatively as first his shirt fell to the floor, then his pants. The masculine proportions of his body struck her as perfectly ideal, his broad shoulders and well-defined chest giving way to narrow hips and long, hard-muscled legs. As he removed his underwear, his thick eight-inch cock rose up to hit his stomach.

Claudia couldn't help but stare. After all those hours in study hall, sneaking glances at him across the room, Levi Schroeder was naked in front of her and she wanted to drink in every inch of the glorious sight he made.

With a cocky grin, Levi knelt between her open legs. Pinning her arms down, he rubbed the swollen crown of his cock all over her body, first teasing her thighs with it, then sliding it between her breasts. Desire bloomed anew in her as she struggled beneath him.

He laughed softly as he dragged his shaft over her mouth. "Do you want this?" he taunted her.

She eagerly opened her mouth but he pulled back. In the flickering light of the movie, she could see the precome gleaming on the tip of his cock. "Please," she whispered.

Levi straddled her neck and pushed his crown into her mouth. She sucked and licked him with every trick she knew, hoping for more of his shaft. Her body was almost humming with the need for stimulation and she longed to touch herself. Yet Levi kept her arms firmly bound over her head as he dipped his penis farther into her mouth, then withdrew.

Claudia twisted with frustration. In the privacy of a bedroom, she would brazenly beg and plead and promise whatever she had to in order to get her way. Here, anyone visiting the men's room might hear their sex noises and come in to find them. Thrusting her breasts higher, she locked her gaze with his in a wordless plea as he slid deep into the welcoming tunnel of her lips and tongue once more.

He moaned. She sensed that he couldn't play this game much longer, that his body was as excited and demanding as her own. Closing her mouth around him, she surrendered to the sensation of his thrusts and the tangy-sweet taste of his precome. Her pelvis felt electric with desire and her stiff nipples ached to be sucked. No one had ever taken possession of her mouth like this and somehow it was even more exciting than if he were tender and considerate.

No sooner had she thought that, than Levi pulled abruptly away and released her arms. Dizzily, she reached between her legs and stroked her swollen clit. But Levi quickly grabbed her hand and pulled her to her feet, leading her down the stairs to the railing.

With one push on her back, he bent her over so she was facing the movie screen while her bottom stuck out toward the balcony seats. It felt like an exceptionally dirty position to be in, as if she were asking to be fucked by any passing stranger. Hot bolts of ecstasy surged to her pussy as all of her old fantasies flooded her mind. Behind her, she heard the rip of a condom foil. Then Levi took her by the hips and positioned his cock against her soft, tingling pussy.

Claudia bit her lip, desperately repressing the urge to cry out. Levi stroked his crown over her folds, teasing her until she tried to thrust back against him in invitation. But once again he held her fast, the weight of his body pinning her against the railing until she was helpless to do anything but wait for the push of his entire shaft inside her.

His hands slid up and fondled her breasts, then slipped down to her aching clit. Circling it with one light, leisurely finger, he whispered in her ear. "Do this while I'm fucking you. Show me how you make yourself come."

Trembling, she replaced his fingers with hers, stimulating her swollen bud. She was so desperate to come again that her clitoris felt as if it were buzzing, her every nerve alive with heat. As she rubbed herself, Levi guided his rigid length into her core. Every inch penetrated her clinging walls, inciting a heat wave of prickling energy that spread from her scalp to her breasts. Levi pulled out, paused, then drove into her again; he began to fuck her steadily now, spearing her sex in a rapid, deep rhythm. Below her, Claudia could see almost all of the audience, who only had to look up to see her face and shoulders over the railing. All of her dreams of being seduced here in the balcony, of being groped and undressed and fucked by a handsome stranger, swelled inside her. She pressed down on her clit as white-hot convulsions swept through her, her pussy squeezing Levi's penis in a tight, throbbing embrace. Levi groaned softly and held her tighter as his hips pumped out his own pleasure inside her.

Claudia took a deep breath as he released her. The movie was still playing and it seemed incredible that the audience had remained oblivious to the sexual storm they had just enjoyed. Levi led her back to the front row, where they collapsed naked into their seats. His black hair was damp with sweat and even in the flickering film light, she could see his flushed cheeks.

He smiled tenderly and stroked back her long hair. "I can't believe we just did that."

She laughed giddily. "It's something I've wanted to do since high school."

"Have sex in the balcony? Or...have sex with me?" He

looked almost shy.

"Both." She leaned forward and kissed him for the first time. "I guess there are some happy endings in real life after all."

Levi lifted up the armrest and she cuddled beneath his outstretched arm, as together they watched one of Hollywood's lost cinematic dreams play out on the giant screen.

# MATTERS OF
# THE HEART

## Tenille Brown

Charlene's choice in the matter would have been to simply stay tucked in her cute little house on Bay Street tonight. That way, she could have avoided it all. But she was hungry and she couldn't control that.

This was how Charlene wound up here.

The bluesy restaurant was convenient, and they had the best seafood in town. She thought she was playing it safe by waiting until after nine when the crowd should have subsided some, but as soon as Charlene reached the door, she saw it. This Valentine's Day was an elaborate, over-the-top mess.

Charlene knew people got silly this time of the year, what with all the hearts and stars in their eyes, but this was ridiculous.

In honor of the occasion, or rather in protest of it, Charlene wore her own cynical VALENTINE'S DAY IS FOR SUCKERS T-shirt with her denim mini, but now, alone in the corner of a crowded romantic restaurant, she wasn't sure she was fooling anyone but herself.

Waiting to order, Charlene realized that she missed him.

So she did what she could to ignore couple after couple holding hands and stealing kisses. She pretended not to see the balloon hearts or hear the soft music. But like a twist out of a bad movie, when Charlene looked to her left, there Clarence was, standing at the bar, leaning over a scotch and soda.

To Charlene's disappointment, Clarence didn't look any worse. Not in the way she had imagined it in her head—that he had aged twenty years over the past couple of months or had somehow gone bald.

If it was possible, Clarence looked better.

And he was standing there alone and running his palm across his toffee forehead, his reddish hair a short puff of curls on his head.

Charlene walked over to him without giving it much thought and tapped him on his shoulder.

"I still have your heart," she said, and right away knew that she should have said *necklace*. She had meant *necklace*.

Clarence turned. He paused in reflection, but quickly appeared to remember what Charlene was referring to.

"Well, the last time I saw it," he said, "my *heart* was in pieces."

Charlene folded her lips. The last time Clarence saw *her*, *she* was in pieces.

"I got it fixed," she said, because she had. For all the good it had done her.

Clarence took another sip of his drink.

"Then keep it," he said, and turned away from her again. Charlene's gaze now rested on Clarence's broad back.

"I don't *want* it," Charlene said, as softly but as firmly as she could. "But I couldn't just throw it out like it meant nothing."

And, in the scheme of things, Charlene knew that the necklace really didn't mean anything, except that then, it had meant everything.

Clarence seemed agitated now, short tempered as he was.

"Really, Charlene, what did it mean?" he asked.

And it occurred to Charlene that they were beginning to feud about something that might have been worth ten bucks tops. It was just some trinket, a silver heart on a silver necklace he had won for her at a carnival. Clarence had pitched a ball. Charlene had cheered him on.

She wore the necklace home that night and left it on when Clarence had stripped her otherwise naked. The heart had danced against her throat as Clarence had stretched her across the living room floor and fucked her so roughly that the carpet burned her back and ass bright red.

Three months later, Charlene still carried the scars from that night. She still saw them and smiled in spite of herself. But she also carried the memory of what happened shortly after, when the necklace had since been placed around the neck of a teddy bear that she wound up throwing at Clarence one heated night.

The teddy bear had survived, but neither the necklace nor their relationship had.

Clarence had walked out—out of her house and out of her life.

Charlene couldn't even remember now whatever foolish thing they had fought about. It had always been some stupid, small thing with them that always seemed to become some big, important thing that they simply couldn't get past.

All she knew was that neither of them had ever had much patience to speak of, but Charlene had expected Clarence to come back, like he always did.

But he didn't. This time Clarence had stayed gone and Charlene had been too stubborn to call and say, "I'm sorry," and

"Will you please come home?"

But Charlene didn't want to explain this to Clarence, so instead she asked, "Have you ordered?"

It was an innocent enough question.

And he gave her an easy enough answer. "Not yet," he said. "I wasn't sure I'd make it past this drink in this crowd."

"I know. Tacky right? I was going to take mine to go."

Clarence took the reins. "Are you still going to or would you like to...maybe...?"

Charlene nodded and shrugged.

"Why not?"

They were seated near the back. Clarence pulled out her chair for her and Charlene didn't oppose it.

She didn't oppose his ordering for her either, his instinctively asking for the crab appetizer and the smoked salmon entrée.

Charlene was convinced it was simply the atmosphere of the restaurant, the dim lights and live band playing soft jazz that made her so relaxed and comfortable. Of course it had to be the frozen Valentini that caused her to smile and lean across the table. And when Clarence rested his hand on top of Charlene's, she let it stay there.

The talk between them was easy, about the yard and how the empty patches were finally filling in. She talked about the dog, though Clarence had never really liked him, and how he was doing just fine.

Charlene added, "I'm doing just fine, too."

And Clarence said, "I'm glad."

Charlene fought urges to talk about the parts of her life that were not fine. Like the fact that she missed him in bed. That sleeping naked just didn't have the same zing without him naked, too, lying next to her.

She felt naked now, the way Clarence was looking at her, looking at her like he knew and remembered, and wanted to tell her the same.

Long after they had emptied their plates and their glasses, long after the crowd had slimmed to just the two of them and the band was packing up, Clarence stood up and extended his hand.

"Walk you to your car?"

Charlene picked up the heart-shaped box of leftover dessert. She nodded and placed her hand in his, a movement as natural as the steps she took walking out of the restaurant.

To anyone lingering in the parking lot, they might have looked exactly like the romantic couple they used to be, holding hands and smiling, but they both knew better.

They stopped at Clarence's car: Charlene leaning against it, Clarence standing in front of her.

"Well," Charlene started, and then she stopped.

She looked down at what she held in her hands. There was the matter of the heart to deal with, the red velvet cake with thick chocolate icing that she held against her middle.

Charlene extended the white box toward Clarence.

"Here, you can it have it," she said. "I don't need it."

"Sure you do. Everybody needs a heart."

"Split it?" Charlene smiled.

"Sure."

Charlene opened the box. Hesitant but bold, she swiped her finger across the thick icing. She slid some into her own mouth first, then went in again and offered some to Clarence next.

He accepted it, his eyes holding hers steady.

His mouth was moist and hot around her fingers. He may as well have been touching Charlene the way the bumps rose on her skin and her nipples hardened, as if a soft wind had come through.

Clarence sucked gently on her finger for much longer than it took to taste the icing and Charlene's body was so aware of him now that she rose on her toes and her eyes fluttered closed with the sensation.

"Sweet," Clarence said, his voice deep.

"Yes, sweet," Charlene said, though she didn't know whether Clarence was referring to the icing or her.

"Tonight was pretty nice." Clarence rocked back and forth on his heels.

"It was," Charlene nodded.

"Romantic," he said.

"Yes."

And this was the point at which she could have chosen to walk away, get into her car and drive off, but more than that, more than anything, Charlene wanted to do something else.

So if tonight were the last time she ever saw him again, she wouldn't remember the silver heart breaking, she would remember this...

Softly at first, Charlene's lips merely rested upon his, as if by accident. And she stepped in close to him, so that the fabric of their shirts rubbed against each other.

Afraid to part her lips farther, and invite Clarence inside her mouth, Charlene remained that way, afraid he wouldn't enter, or if he did, afraid he wouldn't linger.

Clarence removed the conflict of decision from her, and gently pried her lips open with the bittersweet wetness of his tongue.

Laced with sweetness and scotch, his tongue was tart. It was strong and sure like he was, and it moved in and around her mouth.

Pulling away, Charlene breathed in deep. And there it was, the love she had temporarily tucked away. It floated up and out, lingered in the atmosphere only briefly before engulfing her in a misty cloud of rain.

Clarence removed the box from her hands and placed it on the hood of his truck. He gripped both her wrists in one of his hands and raised her arms above her head. He leaned Charlene back against the front of the truck so that her back arched naturally at the center.

Charlene lifted her legs and wrapped them tightly around his hips. His crotch was precisely placed against hers beneath her denim skirt. She felt the head of his enlarged cock rubbing against the fabric of her panties.

She reached down to unzip his pants, but Clarence pulled her hand away.

He was punishing her and she knew it, giving her what she deserved for saying whatever foolish things she had said. Clarence was punishing Charlene so thoroughly and sweetly that tears sprung to her eyes and she bit down on her bottom lip in sweet agony.

Through the fabric of his pants and her panties, Clarence rubbed his cock against her cunt. Charlene's panties were saturated and they clung to the warm square between her legs.

She wanted to beg for release from this torture, she wanted to beg Clarence to give her more, but she knew that if she had him inside her now, she would surely explode, and for that, she wasn't ready.

"I miss you," Clarence growled into her neck.

The words brought her even closer to the edge.

"You left me," Charlene responded in gasps.

"You *made* me," Clarence insisted as he rubbed his cock against her with more force, more urgency.

Charlene didn't continue the debate.

She just said, "Come back. Clarence, come back."

And come Clarence did. He came inside his boxers, against his khaki pants. With a furious spurt, he released his hot seed between Charlene's thighs.

Then, with his fingers, Clarence moved Charlene's panties aside, and gave her two, then three digits. He explored her this way as he gently bit her lips and sucked on her neck. Charlene ground against his hand, holding on to his neck with her own.

Within minutes, Charlene was screaming in the empty parking lot, and Clarence let her fall back onto the hood.

Tonight there was the matter of the heart that lay broken in two on the floor next to the bed. It would cost more to fix it than it was worth, Charlene knew, but she wasn't concerned with that now. Now she was too focused on Clarence standing behind her, maintaining their balance with his hands on her hips as he brought her back against him while he thrust into her.

Clarence waited for Charlene to come before he did. And he *did*, releasing warm wetness on her brown back and ass. They collapsed onto the bed, breath heavy, and kissed before reaching for the covers.

Four months Clarence had been back. Four months Charlene had been falling asleep naked in his arms.

But it was now, it was tonight, as she gripped the covers so tightly that she pulled them toward her, that Charlene realized the heart didn't even matter, that what mattered was her and Clarence, that Clarence had come that night and every night after, and he had stayed.

# SEPTEMBER SONG

## Anna Watson

Ruthie reached down and quickly adjusted her thong. Sol saw her and winked. He was sitting in the armchair, dressed in his suit, resting his cane between his legs. His trousers were tented from his hard-on, and Ruthie wished she could go over there and dive right on it, but he wanted her to finish the chapter. She straightened up, her naked breasts swaying, and continued reading from Duke Ellington's autobiography. "Roaming through the jungle, the jungle of 'ohhs' and 'ahs' searching for a more agreeable noise, I live a life of primitivity with the mind of a child and an unquenchable thirst for sharps and flats." She stopped, looking closely at Sol. His eyes were closed and one hand had left the cane and was resting on his hard cock. She wiggled with impatience as he murmured for her to go on. She was new to thong wearing, and it certainly took some getting used to. Still, what better way to spend a rainy afternoon than listening to old jazz on the stereo, reading in the near nude to your sweet and sexy older lover? She licked her finger, turned the page and kept reading.

Ruthie and Sol had met a year ago when Ruthie started giving away clothes. She got the idea when a fellow secretary at Harvard was reminiscing about the free clothes bin they used to have at a food co-op in Allston. It had been one of the first places people on the street or with very little money would go when they got into town. Ruthie had heard other people talk about the bin, but this time something clicked, and she said to herself, "Well, I can do that. I can certainly give away clothes." It sounded nice. Useful. And it really was very easy.

She started by cleaning out her own drawers and supplementing with things she bought cheap at the thrift store. Where to give them away, though, that was a bit daunting at first. The co-op in Allston was long gone. Then she found Food Not Bombs, a free meal served outside around the city during the summer and at a church during the winter, and things fell into place. All she had to do was show up with her truck full of clothes, and people who came to eat flocked around her. She soon figured out the kinds of things they needed: socks, underwear, warm things in the winter, sandals and T-shirts later on. There were people who cared about style and others who just wanted something, anything, to put on.

She branched out a little and sometimes went to Costco to buy toothbrushes in bulk, and dental floss, ChapStick, tampons, nail clippers, lotion. People really appreciated that. She started to get to know some of the regulars. At first, people were a little wary, but when they saw she was going to keep showing up, they relaxed. She liked talking to folks about what they would wear if they had the money, and then trying to find it for them, cheap or free. She started getting clothes from a Quaker organization and people she knew began coming by with donations once the word got out about what she was doing. Some of the clothes she had to throw out, but the rest she cleaned and mended and put out. She was especially proud when she found a leather jacket for Sol, even if it did have a small stain and an even smaller tear.

"I have sartorial sense," Sol told her when they first met. He was right there, going carefully through the clothes. He wouldn't take just anything. He was a big old man with clear gray eyes and a hawk nose, around seventy-five. "The stuff Ben used to bring had been going down in quality," he told her. "Can you get some good quality stuff?"

Ben was her predecessor, now in a home. Sol and some of the other guys who came to the meals went to visit him when they could. It was fortuitous, Sol told her, that she'd shown up when she had. Who would have brought clothes with Ben gone?

"He did it as long as he could, but he got old," Sol said, leaning on his cane. "Like me." He looked at her with those gray eyes and smiled. He had all his own teeth. Sol was old, but he was pretty well preserved. She told him so, and he kept smiling, taking her in, leaning on his cane, one of those metal ones with four feet. Then he shuffled off to get dessert. Sol had a sweet tooth, something Ruthie now knew about him. After a few weeks, she knew quite a bit about him, and he had started helping her out, standing beside her holding the sock bag, for example. When they bumped shoulders or hips, Sol smiled and said, "Excuse me, young lady."

"This is a good story," said Sol one evening. "Let me tell you this story." They were sitting together on a bench while Ruthie ate. When she'd first started at Food Not Bombs, she didn't think she should eat, since she could afford food and wanted to leave it for people who couldn't, but then she started eating to keep Sol company and to not seem standoffish. The food was usually some kind of vegetable curry, with brown rice, salad and bread.

Sometimes a macaroni dish. Sol put down his empty paper plate and looked to see if there was any dessert today. Nope.

"I was about fourteen, and I had saved up enough money to get a radio for myself. My sister had one, but she didn't always like me hanging around. I went to Jordan's and got a good one. I was proud of that radio. Right after I got it, I was listening to Bob Hope, and at the time, hemlines had been going up, you know, women's skirts. And so he's telling jokes, patter, and he says, 'Well, folks, the way I see it, if ladies' skirts get any shorter, they'll have more hair to comb and two more cheeks to powder!' and just then, the radio went dead. I jumped out of my chair—I thought my brand new radio was broken. But of course, they'd pulled him off the air. I heard he got a fine."

Ruthie was laughing hard, snorting, really. "I can't believe that!" she said. "Did you get it?"

"Get it? Of course I got it! I was fourteen years old!" He looked offended.

"Well, some people are still pretty naïve when they're fourteen," said Ruthie. She put her hand on his arm and left it there. She liked hearing about Sol's childhood. By this time, she knew many details of his past, and he was telling her about his health now, too. Declining. If he had only known, he told her. Old age is no picnic.

Sol had a special kind of smell. It was his clothes, Ruthie thought, because in general he seemed pretty clean. Clean shaven. The smell, dusty and metallic, came from being outside in the city all the time, sitting here and there on the bus, reading the paper someone had left, working the crossword, looking in the trash for bottles and cans. He was always out, always walking around. Slowly, of course, with the cane. He walked downtown to go to the doctor—he had Medicaid, thank god—and then he walked to various meals. There were meals every night, somewhere. Ruthie couldn't get to all of them, but she brought clothes out at least twice a week. Sol was usually there.

After a while, she started taking home some of his clothes to wash and mend. Shoving them into the washing machine, the smell would surprise her, and she would smile. She had the feeling that if she were to put her nose right up to one of the benches on the Cambridge Common it would smell just like Sol.

One night, after she'd been doing clothes for about three months, some of the Food Not Bombs volunteers asked her out with them. Sol had already gone home—he had a rent-controlled efficiency somewhere—so Ruthie said yes. The volunteers were all really young, kind of a wild bunch, with blue hair and piercings. There was a lot of flirting and personal drama, but not with her. They were into each other, and someone like her, nearing forty, wasn't so relevant.

"So what's going on with you and Sol?" asked the white boy who wore his hair in two little antennae. "I saw you slipping him a box of oatmeal. People are talking."

Ruthie looked at his shoes. That kind of shoe was very popular and didn't often get donated. "We're buds, I guess," she said.

"Oh," said the Grateful Dead girl. "He's such an old dear. He's one of my very favorites!"

Then everybody started talking about their favorites and after they had made their lists and comparisons, they went on to hash over the rumor that one of the women who had been coming to the meal for years was really a millionaire. The black kid who shaved his head kept saying, "What I want to know is, how come she needs a free meal?" Nobody seemed to know.

The next time Ruthie saw Sol, she asked him out for ice cream, which was something they never had at Food Not Bombs. When the clothes had been picked over and put away,

Sol hauled himself up into the cab of her truck and they drove to Toscanini's in Central Square.

"I'm paying," said Ruthie, and Sol accepted in the gracious way he had. They sat at a tiny wrought-iron table and Ruthie had her usual, grape nut pudding, and Sol had coffee. Sol's lips, thin and expressive, looked good covered with coffee ice cream, and then he licked it off and that looked good, too. Ruthie leaned forward, showing off her breasts. These days, she'd been wearing low-cut shirts whenever she saw him. She just felt it was something nice she could provide for him. "You're a beautiful man, Sol," she said.

"Ruthie, I knew you were a *mensch* the first time I saw you," he replied, taking in her cleavage. He was wearing his leather jacket, of course, had been wearing it since she'd gotten it for him. She'd never seen him take it off. At his feet was a well-worn plastic KB Toys bag, opaque, with handles, filled with cans, she thought, and maybe a newspaper. "You know what a *mensch* is?" He was always quizzing her on Yiddish, and was very interested in her upbringing as a Christmas Jew. "You really believed in Santa Claus?" he would ask. "Come on, your parents let you have a Christmas tree?" Sol himself had been born and raised in an Orthodox family in Dorchester. "I'm the youngest of six," he had told her, "three brothers, deceased, two sisters, both alive, both with their own *tsurus*."

"Sorrows," she translated before he could ask.

"You're a smart woman," he told her.

After a while, Ruthie wanted Sol to come home with her. She didn't have any roommates, and they could be alone. This was a very alone kind of thing, anyway. She felt awkward talking to her friends about Sol. When she tried, Trish, a friend from art school who was usually pretty open-minded, said, "You have a crush on an *old homeless guy*? Are you *okay?*"

"He lives somewhere," muttered Ruthie, but she kept her mouth shut after that.

Sol didn't want to come over at first. He had his life and his routines. The Brookline McDonald's for coffee with his buddies in the afternoon (it was no good, but it was cheap). The various free meals, the places he went to meet people, hang out and *kibbitz*. Going to Ruthie's, keeping company with a young woman—he wasn't used to it, he told her.

Ruthie wanted to do things for him, cook for him, buy little things. Things he couldn't buy for himself, like a boom box so he could listen to Artie Shaw. She was worried it might hurt his pride, but then again, Sol seemed to be in the market for a little ministering to these days. He hadn't been feeling too well. The pain in his belly. The pain in his feet. The stuff going on with his prostate. One day Ruthie asked him over for supper and said she wouldn't take no for an answer. He showed up with a bottle of wine. He left his bag beside the door. He took off his coat and Red Sox cap. He had more hair than she'd thought he would, gray and greasy. He was wearing a really pretty sweater.

"Did you get that off Ben?" she asked, and Sol said yes and showed her there was a hole under the arm. She told him to take it off so she could fix it. When she took it from him, their hands touched, and she squeezed, gently. He squeezed back. The mend job came out a little crooked, but he appreciated the effort.

"How little we know, how much to discover..." he sang as she got the food ready, standing in her kitchen, leaning on his cane. The crooners, the big bands, that's what he liked. That's what he bought the radio for when he was fourteen. Beautiful ballads like "Maybe You'll Be There." For supper, they had chicken, rice, salad, then ice cream for dessert.

"I like pastries, too," said Sol. Ruthie smiled. She leaned over and licked the ice cream—chocolate—from his lips.

"I've been wanting to do that ever since Toscanini's," she said. He sat very still. "What's wrong?" She left her chair and knelt beside him on the floor and put her head in his lap. At once she felt his big hand on her hair, and he stroked and stroked. She moved between his legs and pressed up against his chest and belly and crotch. He hadn't put the sweater back on because the heat was messed up in her apartment, and it was sweltering in there. Under his thin white T-shirt, she could feel his skin, his nipples, sagging some, but so what? We all sag eventually. She put her hand on his belly and felt the hair around his belly button. She moved her hand and Sol sighed.

"It feels good when you rub," he said softly, so she rubbed there, and then she rubbed lower. "You'd better stop. I don't know what will happen." She looked up at his face. He was an old man. His cheeks were red and his eyes watered. "I'm an old man," he said, and Ruthie said, "So can you still get it up?" Sol closed his eyes in what Ruthie thought at first was pained embarrassment—he didn't like it when women at the meal swore or talked dirty—but then he started laughing, so Ruthie took off her shirt.

Ruthie had big tits. Double D's. It had taken her a long time to make peace with them, just about all her life. They were out of proportion with the rest of her—she was five-four and slender—and when she was younger, she'd hated them. Trying to get guys to pay attention to something other than her breasts had been such an ordeal. She'd spent a long time in baggy shirts. But now she felt fine about how she looked. Having cleavage was nice, and obviously Sol thought so, too. "Baby, you are stacked but good," he said as he reached for her bra. "You do this, I can't manipulate it anymore."

"But you did once upon a time," she said, undoing the clasp

for him. "You had them begging for it." Sol smiled, but kept his mouth shut. Some things were private. Ruthie came up close and rubbed her breasts on his chest and belly. She wanted him to take off his shirt, but he wasn't so sure.

"You might not want to see this," he said.

"What?" she asked. "A scar? A blemish?" He shrugged and started to get out of the shirt. She helped him pull it over his head. The hair under his arms was white. She wanted to lick it. She was big into licking.

"I'm an old man," he said again and she laughed.

"I'm going to lick you under the arm," she said, and she did, which meant her tits were banging up against him. She pushed them together and rubbed them all over his mouth and nose and eyes. She felt his arms come around her and he pulled her half onto him. He slid his thumbs under the waistband of her jeans and struggled to get them down. She helped him and now she was naked.

"Put your arm here," she said, pulling it between her legs. She moved down his arm until his hand was there. He cupped her pussy and gently rubbed her slit, pushing up, sliding back, then dabbling two fingers in her hole. Like that, she couldn't tell they were all crippled up with arthritis.

"Ah, Jesus," said Sol, leaning way back in his chair as she held herself up on his shoulders and moved around on his hand. "So wet." He grabbed for her nipple with his mouth and when she leaned close they started to overbalance. Sol stopped fingering her and she got worried he was going to get freaked out and want to stop.

"Come to bed," she said, slipping off him. He had to pee first, and then he sat on the bed and looked shy. Ruthie straddled him and pushed him back, easy.

"I don't care if you get hard or not," she said, trying to take off his pants. Finally, he let her. They lay on their sides, facing each other, and she kissed him and licked him all over. He was very white, flabby, but hard underneath, and she grabbed handfuls of his ass and just squeezed. His dick jumped in the bush of gray hair—it was nice and plump. She held it and it jumped again. Sol said, "Jesus," and started pumping. Ruthie wanted to ask how long it had been since he'd last fucked, but it didn't seem very polite. It seemed a little triumphant. She took his hand and brought it to his dick and they played with it together until he was hard. She grabbed a rubber from the drawer in her nightstand, got it open, and put it on with her mouth, a little trick she and Trish had practiced on a lavender dildo a few years back. He held her head and seemed to be settling back to get blown, but she didn't want to be down there right now, so she disengaged and slid back up his body. For her, it had been a while. His dick slipped in so sweetly, and the two of them started moaning and talking.

"Fuck me, fuck me," said Sol, and she opened her eyes in surprise. She'd never heard him say an obscenity. She tried to keep as much weight off his body as she could, but now he was grabbing at her and pushing up. They fucked like that until he came and fell out, soft. She just kept going on top of it. She liked the feel of it underneath her, sometimes hitting her just right. He moved his hips, helping her and smiling. She came and rolled off, then fell asleep, listening to him snore.

# SAVED

## Cassandra Carr

Honey, are you happy?"

It was the hardest question she'd ever asked her husband, but she had to do something. So much was at stake—their marriage, her happiness. She could no longer afford to pretend everything was all right.

He looked at her, his expressive eyebrows furrowing the slightest bit. "Of course I'm happy. Why?"

After biting her lip briefly, she continued, her heart in her throat. "What I mean is, are you happy with our sex life? Is it everything you'd like it to be?"

She knew her marriage was in trouble when she realized she'd rather read than make love. For the past couple of years, things had gotten pretty dull in the sex department. Sure, she and her husband still loved each other, but just as in many marriages, they weren't exactly burning up the sheets.

"Well, I think everybody wishes they could have sex more often, but it's not realistic with how many hours we both work and how tired we are by the end of the day," he answered. "Other than that, though…" He shrugged. Then he narrowed his green eyes at her, assessing. She'd fallen in love with his eyes before anything else about him and they still held so much power over her that she squirmed under his scrutiny. "Why are you asking? Are you not happy?"

"No, it's not that," she hastened to reassure him, though she was afraid if he balked at her suggestions she might become truly unhappy. Right now she was more…restless. She bit her lip. "I just think there are some things we could do to, I don't know…spice things up around here."

Her husband, whom she'd been attracted to not only for his good looks—dark-brown hair, olive skin, full mouth—but also for his steadiness of character, had become downright strait-laced as he'd gotten older. He liked sex, sure, but had never shown any real inclination to explore sexual boundaries.

She, on the other hand, had become more comfortable with her body and her sexuality and was tired of squelching those feelings, afraid he would think she was some sort of deranged pervert. He'd never given her that indication; he was always loving and supportive, and she was sure it was her own para-noia and insecurities talking, but she hadn't felt like she could take that chance.

To help combat her feelings of loneliness, she'd turned to books. During one of her frequent trips to the bookstore she'd discovered erotic romance. While perusing the aisles looking for something a little different, her gaze fell on the cover of a book and she couldn't tear her eyes away: one woman was sand-wiched between two hunky, drop-dead gorgeous men.

Fascinated, she reached for the book and pulled it off the shelf, surreptitiously looking around to see if anyone had seen her take it. Then she scooted over to a chair nearby and flipped the book over, reading the back cover blurb. Her mouth fell open—it was about a woman who had a ménage à trois relationship! A *committed* ménage à trois relationship! She'd never heard of such a thing. Did people actually *do* that?

She took the book home, hidden in a pile of other books, and read it in secret. It was a page-turner, filled with hot men and even hotter sex. She found herself getting aroused as she read about the men with their hands all over the woman, doing things to her that she'd heard about but had never even dreamed of doing: anal sex, toys—even double penetration.

That book opened up a whole new world for her and she started reading more and more. She went online and ordered a half dozen others—some straight erotic romance, others with different themes—spanking, BDSM. You name it, she wanted to read about it. After a while it became impossible to hide her growing obsession.

Erotic romance novels turned out to be the cheapest therapy she'd ever found. They helped her figure something out: through them she could learn about new and different ways to achieve passion, to heighten intimacy. That's how she'd gotten the courage to speak up today: she was hoping her husband would see there was a whole world of new things available to them if he was willing to step outside his comfort zone.

He looked intrigued by her suggestion to liven things up, which she figured was a good sign. Now she needed to see how he reacted when she showed him the things she'd purchased online to help them explore new facets of their sexuality. She'd gotten some good lube, a butt plug, a paddle, a blindfold, handcuffs, nipple clamps and a vibrator. She didn't plan to bring everything out at once—that might scare him off, but she figured she'd better get everything while she still had the nerve.

Now then, where to start?

She thought back to the items she'd picked up, and then reached into the drawer, pulling out the blindfold and handcuffs. Those were probably the safest, least threatening things she had. Now, should she tell him she wanted to be tied up or should she offer to tie him up? Glancing at his face, she went with her first instinct. "Would you like to handcuff me to the bed, blindfold me and have your way with me?" She gave him a smile and ran her hand down her front between her breasts. His eyes followed, and he inhaled deeply.

"Yeah, I could do that."

She went for it. "Want to try it now?" Lying back on the bed, she handed him the cuffs.

He smiled and reached to pull off her shirt and bra. "Put your hands over your head." He fastened the cuffs to the headboard and looked down at her. "Comfortable?"

"Fine." They weren't the most comfortable things in the world, but she wasn't about to complain. This was progress!

Leaning down to kiss her, he said, "I kind of like having you at my mercy."

"Do your worst."

Slipping the blindfold over her eyes, he answered, "I will." She doubted he could do anything that would scare her the least bit, but she was willing to see where this would go. Already she could feel her panties growing moist, and that by itself was a positive sign.

He left the bed and she heard rustling. She assumed he was undressing, but when the bed shifted again and all she felt were his hands on her, she couldn't be sure. He wrapped his hands around her hips and then glided upward until he reached the underside of her breasts. Skimming along the sensitive skin with the tips of his thumbs, he swept back and forth a few times. She arched, trying to push her breasts farther into his hands, but he pushed her back down gently.

"Shhh..."

She whimpered, and he leaned down to press a kiss to her lips. Trailing his mouth down her jaw to her neck, he placed nibbling kisses all the way to her collarbone. Having her arms held over her head and the blindfold on definitely made a difference in how it felt when he touched her. Every other sense was heightened, and her position forced her breasts to thrust upward.

Running a hand down her stomach, he latched on to her right breast with his hot mouth and began to suckle. His hand delved between her thighs and he pressed the palm into her damp mound before plunging two fingers into her sex. She let out a plaintive moan at the sudden contact.

But as he continued to work her, she found that it felt good but wasn't bringing her over the edge. Even being forced to rely on her other senses wasn't heightening her excitement level enough to induce orgasm. After what felt like an eternity where she had to give him credit for keeping at it, she finally came. He removed the blindfold and uncuffed her hands a short time later. Smiling up at him, she touched his cheek and kissed him softly.

"What about you?"

"I'm okay, but if you want to help me out, I won't stop you..." He smiled at her.

Using her hand, she brought him off quickly. After a few moments, she yawned. "You look pretty tired," he remarked.

"I am."

"Why don't you get some sleep? I'm going to go watch a movie on the computer. I'll come to bed in a few hours."

"Okay." She rolled over and tried to get comfortable, but couldn't. Now she was riled up. She felt unfulfilled from the encounter and wanted to come again. Turning back toward the nightstand, she quietly opened the drawer and withdrew the vibrator. She'd experimented with it a few times, not wanting to fumble with it if he ever agreed to use it. She knew she could make herself orgasm with it quickly.

Pulling the sheet and blankets up around her, she snuck the vibrator under them and worked it into her pussy, turning it on low. Immediately the buzzing action caused her sex to clench, and her knees bent as she threw her head back. She knew she wasn't far from climax, and she turned the toy up to the medium level.

It only took about thirty seconds before she felt the beginnings of her orgasm working its way down her spine. Curling her toes, she felt her entire body tense as the spasms began in earnest. Biting down on her lip to keep from crying out, she rode out the waves of pleasure until they finally subsided, then sank bank onto the mattress. Only allowing herself a scant moment of postorgasmic bliss, she got up and washed the vibrator and hid it in the drawer again. After settling herself into bed again, she fell into a deep, dreamless sleep.

A few weeks later she approached her husband again. "Would you like to try some other toys I picked up?"

He looked hesitant at first but agreed.

She knew he loved her breasts, so she brought out the nipple clamps. "What are those?" He looked genuinely perplexed and she had to stifle the urge to laugh. She explained their use and his eyes widened. "And you *want* to do that?"

"After you get used to them it's kind of a dull pain, which is supposed to be pretty erotic, and when you take them off it feels pretty good, too, some say. I thought you might like to see my nipples clamped—a lot of guys seem to get off on it."

"Why?"

"I don't know. It's like they've marked their woman as theirs or something."

He smirked and one ebony-colored eyebrow rose. "Marked my woman?"

"Yes. Do you want to try them or not?"

"I don't know. Do you?"

She sighed again. Apparently she was going to have to take the lead in the entire process, even though she really wanted to be submissive and let him take charge. It didn't look like that was going to happen anytime soon, though. "Sure." Taking his hand, she showed him how to attach the clamps. "You'll have to suck my nipples pretty hard to get them to stand up enough so the clamp can latch on to them." He smiled then. "Yeah, I thought you'd like that." Maybe there was hope for them yet...

After making her nipples stand at attention, he fastened the clamps and adjusted them until they felt just as she'd expected: a dull ache. She was surprised by how much the little bite of pain ratcheted up her arousal, though. She fell to her knees and began to unbutton his pants. She needed to taste him.

"What are you doing?"

"I want to taste you."

"Taste me? But you never want to—"

"I do now." Before he could say anything more, she took him into her mouth as far as she could. He gasped and grabbed her hair before backing off. She pulled her mouth off of him long enough to say, "No, don't do that. I like it when you hold my head; guide me in how to pleasure you."

He looked dubious, but cupped a hand on the back of her neck. Using the other to hold his cock, he guided it back into her mouth and she moaned. He was right; she'd never been a fan of giving head, but with her nipples clamped and on her knees in front of him, it seemed natural.

She continued to suck and nibble at his penis, and soon he began to thrust into her mouth. He was still holding back, though, and so she grabbed both cheeks of his ass and squeezed, pulling him closer to her and his dick farther into her mouth.

"Honey, I'm gonna come," he panted, trying to move away from her, but she held fast. "You're gonna swallow? Oh, god..." With just a few thrusts more his cock began to pulse and then filled her mouth with his warm, salty essence. She drank it down, shocked by how greedy she was for his come.

After a moment, he withdrew from her mouth and sank back onto the bed. She crawled up beside him and snuggled in, removing the clamps and releasing a brief hiss as the blood returned. "If I'd known putting nipple clamps on would inspire that, I would've done it a long time ago," he mused.

Raising herself up on her elbow, she looked down at him. "I have a few other things that I'd like to try, and I think they'll turn me on just like the clamps did." Walking her fingers up his chest, she smiled.

One eyebrow went up. "Oh, yeah? Like what? Show me." She turned and took out everything else, figuring she might as well go for broke while he was in a receptive mood. His eyes widened when he saw the paddle and the butt plug. "You want me to spank you? I don't know if I can do that—I don't want to hurt you."

"You won't hurt me. There's a difference between an erotic spanking and punishment."

"I guess so..." He sounded unconvinced, but she could explain more about that later. Right now she decided it was a good time to show him how the plug worked, since he was staring at it like it was a poisonous snake.

"Do you know what this is?" At the shake of his head, she continued. "It's a butt plug."

He immediately tensed. "What the hell do you use *that* for? I can tell you one thing—no one's going anywhere near my ass with that."

She couldn't help but laugh. "It isn't for you, it's for me."

"But why?"

"Because if you're willing to, I'd like to try anal sex."

"Anal sex? Are you kidding me?"

"Hear me out." Taking a deep breath, she began. "I've been reading up on it online. It's supposed to be really pleasurable for both of us." When he didn't say anything she took it as a good sign and plowed on. "You know how you like it when I squeeze you when you're inside me? Well, apparently it feels that tight, or even tighter, for you. And there are a lot of nerve endings, just like in my pussy, so it feels really good to me, too."

"I don't know..."

"Look: try it, just a few times. If you really don't like it we don't have to try anymore. And I need to wear the plug a few times before we do anything, anyway. That'll make it easier for me to take you."

"If this is what you want, I'll try it. I want you to be happy."

She supposed that would have to be good enough for now, though she had a feeling that once he knew what it felt like to have sex that way he'd be a fan for life.

"Can you help me put in the plug?" He needed to be comfortable with touching her ass before any of this would work, so this was a good place to start.

"Yeah. What should I do?"

She showed him how to lube it up and then how to drizzle more lube on the pucker itself. "Now start pushing it in. I'll give you instructions if I need you to go slower or anything." She'd used the plug a few times herself and knew it wasn't painful but she wanted him to see that. He placed the tip of the plug at her opening and began to push, ever so slowly. "That's good, keep going..." she urged him. Soon the plug was seated firmly in her ass. She smiled at him as he met her eyes, obvious concern clouding his. "It doesn't hurt. Really. It feels...full."

"I'll take your word for it."

After a few hours in which she got nothing done because of the strange feeling of having her plug in, she removed it and began to plan the next phase of their exploration. She decided to send him an email with her fantasy written out. That way, she wouldn't have to voice the whole thing and he could read and ponder it in his own time.

*Honey, I know I've asked a lot of you over the past couple of weeks. But I really think this is good for us. I hope you feel the same. I want to tell you about a fantasy I have that I'd like you to fulfill if you're willing...*

*The thought of having a man dominate me turns me on. I think it's because I have so many responsibilities, between work, home, etc, that it's nice to think of putting my pleasure into someone else's hands. Maybe you can't understand that, but that's okay. You don't have to; all you have to do is accept it and help me bring to life what I think will be a great sexual experience for both of us.*

*I would like you to pick some night in the next week or so for this fantasy. I don't want you to think about it too much. Just do it and see how it makes you feel. Can you do that? I love you!*

*Here's what my fantasy is: I want you to come to me and tell me you want to see me in the bedroom. Don't say anything more; just go in the bedroom. When I arrive, order me to my knees and then put your cock in my mouth without saying another word. Fuck my mouth—hold the sides of my head, tilt my mouth to your liking, whatever feels good to you. But don't come. That will be later.*

*Then, after I've sucked your cock for a while, order me to get over your lap. Once I'm there you'll push up my skirt and pull down my panties to expose my bare bottom. (I'll wear skirts every day until you choose to fulfill the fantasy to make things easier.) Then you'll start to spank me with your hand. Spank me as long as you want to, and then tell me to stand up, but don't let me pull my panties up.*

*Order me to go to the nightstand and get the paddle and then bring it back to you. I will, and you will then put me over your lap again. You'll begin to paddle my bare ass and continue until you think I've been spanked enough. You are in charge here, completely—I don't want you to ask me if I think you've spanked me enough. I want to know that you're going to spank me for as long as you want to, and there's nothing I can do about it.*

*When you're finished spanking me, order me to undress and get on the bed on my hands and knees so you can fuck my ass. Then you'll undress, too, and put on a condom. Lube it up good, and be sure you put lube on me, too. When you're ready, start pushing into me. I'll give you verbal cues about whether I need you to slow down, keep moving forward, whatever.*

*When you're in all the way, you'll fuck me just like you do when you're in my pussy. While you're inside me, I'll feel how hot my ass is from your spanking, plus all the other sensations, and I predict I'll come pretty hard. However, I don't want you to stop until you've come, too, no matter how long it takes (which I don't think will be long!).*

*So that's my fantasy.*

*Will you do it?*

* * *

She sent the email and then rubbed her clammy hands on her jeans. Now she just had to wait to see if he would go through with it. She didn't have to wait long.

The next night he came to her as she was sitting in the living room, reading, and said quietly, "I'd like to see you in the bedroom." She glanced up, surprised, but his face betrayed no emotion. He hadn't mentioned the email or whether or not he'd be willing to fulfill her fantasy, so she wasn't quite sure what to expect.

She padded after him into the bedroom. He shut the door and turned to her, his formerly green eyes nearly black with desire. "On your knees." Lifting his hands to her shoulders, he pushed her down. As soon as her knees hit the floor he began to fumble with the zipper of his pants—the only indication he was feeling as nervous as she was. He pulled out his cock, and her eyes widened. Somehow it seemed like he was harder than she'd ever seen him. Cupping the back of her head, he guided his erection to her lips and slid home—all the way to the back of her throat.

Tilting her head up, he took hold of her face in a strong grip with both hands and began to thrust in and out of her mouth. She held on as best she could as the head of his cock sank into her throat again and again. He'd never pushed this far into her mouth and she had to concentrate to keep from gagging on his length. She looked up at him. His expression was feral, intense. A shiver stole through her, and she finally understood what it was like to be dominated. She wanted more.

He wrapped his arms around her head and forced her onto his cock until her nose was tickled by the coarse hair at the base of him. While he was holding her there, she heard him emit a hoarse growl and her pussy gushed with moisture. Finally he released her and tilted her head back even farther, so that he was practically straddling her face as he continued to saw his dick in and out of her mouth. Her jaw was beginning to hurt, but there was no way she would break this spell.

After long moments he stepped back. His breathing was heavy and his skin was flushed. It all added to the mystique of the situation and her pussy clenched with need.

He sat down on the bed. "Over my knees." She crawled over his lap, trepidation setting in. She'd never been spanked before, and she'd told him to spank her as long as he wanted. How long would that be? How much would it hurt? Further thoughts flew out of her head as her skirt was raised and flipped over onto her back. Then he hooked his fingers in the waistband of her panties and pulled them all the way down to her knees. She gulped, waiting.

The first spank was such a shock that she jumped and yelped. "No sound!" he commanded, his voice exuding deadly calm. "Or I'll gag you." Had he been reading her books? Her sex fluttered and she was afraid she'd come just from his spanking. He began to spank her again. He alternated cheeks for a while, spanking her harder than she'd thought he would. After a while he concentrated on the area where her ass met her thighs and she hissed out a breath. That hurt!

When her bottom and the tops of her thighs were completely covered and she felt like a million bees were stinging her ass, he stopped. "Get up, but leave your panties down." Remembering that she still had a spanking with the paddle coming, she gulped. "Go get the paddle out of the drawer and bring it to me. I think your ass still needs a lot of spanking. You've been a very naughty girl."

She gasped, unable to believe how much his words were turning her on. Waddling over to the nightstand with her panties still down at her knees, she took the paddle out of the bottom drawer

and brought it back to him. He took it and said, "Back over my
knees. I'm not done with you yet—not by a long shot." She practically threw herself back over his lap, not wanting to get punished
further for hesitating, and he began to paddle her immediately.

Biting her lip, she tried to keep quiet, but the spanking was
far more painful than she'd thought it would be, and soon she
was letting out a little grunt each time the paddle landed. She
could feel his still rock-hard cock bouncing against her hip as he
continued to paddle her, and she knew she wasn't the only one
being affected by their little game.

She was close to tears before he stopped spanking her. "Do
you know what happens to naughty girls after they get spanked?"
Figuring it was a rhetorical question, she didn't answer. The
paddle came down hard on her thighs and she jumped, letting
out an involuntary squeal. "Answer me."

"N-no, sir," she stammered. He was going to kill her if he
didn't fuck her soon. She had never been so aroused in her
entire life.

"They get their asses fucked." He squeezed her red-hot cheeks
and she bit her lip against the pain. "Undress and then get up
on your hands and knees on the bed." She followed his instructions, watching as he removed his own clothes and sheathed
his raging erection. "Eyes forward." Where had this man come
from? And how long would he stay? she wondered.

Soon she felt his hands spreading her cheeks and then he
was spreading the lube on her and in her. After a moment an
odd feeling of pressure began as he eased the head of his cock
into her ass. She breathed in and out and pushed back against
him. He rocked his dick in and out of her passage until she felt
the tight ring of muscle give, and then he was inside. His voice
was strained as he said, "You've taken about half of me. Can
you handle more?"

"Yes," she whispered, and he groaned.

"Feels so fucking good..."

"I know. For me, too." That seemed to make something snap inside of him, and he pushed the rest of the way in, his thighs bumping up against her punished cheeks.

"You okay?" He was panting and she imagined he was trying to hold off his orgasm.

"Yes, just move, please. I need you to move."

He did, pulling back and then pushing in over and over. Reaching between her legs, he massaged her clit and that was all it took for her to go off like a rocket. When she began to clench around him, he went over the edge, too, letting out a low groan as he spilled himself inside her. After long seconds he pulled out of her and went to the bathroom to dispose of the condom. She stayed where she was, unsure of what to do next.

Returning, he pulled her down beside him and nuzzled her neck. "What a little vixen you are! Thank you for opening my eyes, honey. I never knew sex could be like this. I just came harder than I ever have in my entire life."

"You're welcome," she murmured. "I did, too. I'm pretty sure you made me see stars." Smiling bigger than she had in a long, long time, she asked, "So when can we do it again?"

He laughed and the fire of lust flashed in his eyes. She felt tears welling up—grateful, happy tears. "When are you going to be a bad girl again?"

Releasing a snort of laughter herself, she answered, "As often as possible."

"Then I think you have a lot of spankings coming to you, naughty girl."

"And a lot of other stuff, too?"

"Oh, yeah—a *lot* of other stuff."

# FOR THE VERY FIRST TIME

### Rachel Kramer Bussel

D ean and I are snuggled on my couch, half watching TV, half
feeling each other up. We've been dating for two months,
a long time for me to go without sex, but I'm comfortable with
the way the night is going. We've already decided that he'll sleep
over and spend the weekend. He's done it before, and I've stayed
at his place, but this night feels more momentous. I know something is going to change, and I feel that charge of something
new and thrilling, of anticipation, in the air.

We watch some cheesy sitcom, and then I move to sit on his
lap. I don't usually do that with guys, because I'm six feet tall,
and even when they're tall (Dean's just two inches shorter than
me), it quickly becomes clear I'm not some petite little thing
who can fit cozily on their laps. They have to commit to it, to
make an effort, to really want it. I'm not offended when guys
prefer side-by-side cuddling, but this time it feels right to be
sitting on Dean's lap, feeling his hardness beneath me.

I'm getting so turned on I don't even mind that it's not,

actually, the most comfortable position. I'm slowly sinking into him, our bodies merging. If I shift a little, his breath catches the back of my neck, making me tingle. Dean doesn't seem to mind, and his hand lazily plays with the waistband of my new pink mesh panties through the silky fabric of my gray dress. I'm waiting, eager, practically climbing the walls. My desire is like that much of the time: content to lie dormant, until it makes itself known and won't take no for an answer. Of course I've used my assortment of sex toys during the time we've been dating, and the four months before that when I was lazily single, not eager to seek out someone new, content to wait and see. But six months is a long time, and I'm horny and oh-so-ready. I've been trying to be the girl here, the one who waits to get seduced, the one who lets the man feel manly by making the first move, even though that's not normally my style. I don't know if I really believe in all that stuff, but it's sort of like religion, to me; if there's a chance that believing is worth it, I'm in, and I've found that even the most enlightened men can easily fall prey to being the macho man, the seducer. I'm always willing to try something new, and from the times I've felt Dean's cock through his pants, it's one worth waiting for, though by now I've waited long enough.

We met just when I'd been ready to consider looking up an ex for a roll in the hay. I saw Dean and simply couldn't look away. He was so stunning that I couldn't help but go over to him after hearing him sing at my local café, where we're sometimes treated to the likes of a Shawn Colvin or John Prine, but more often get the up-and-comers. I don't generally bother with younger men, but Dean's voice and delivery said to me "old soul." Too many guys in their twenties and even thirties are so cocky they think every woman, even those totally out of their league, was put on earth just to blow them. That type will hit on me, but shrink away when I demand a mere modicum of commitment.

But Dean was different. He was handsome, but not so perfect that he was arrogant, at least from what I could tell as I watched him strumming his guitar. So many performers have that ego thing down pat, but he had the shy, earnest look of a busker, one who was more comfortable in the bowels of a subway station than on a stage surrounded by drinks and laughter and flirting. It was almost like he was singing these soulful, tender, beautiful songs to himself, with his eyes closed, his body thrown into each song. He launched into a Richard Thompson cover, "Beeswing." He didn't try to do the accent, but he sang with all his heart. When he got to the end, the line, "Well I wouldn't want her any other way," I could tell he was thinking of his own version of that song's eccentric heroine, and I found that I wasn't jealous of his girl who got away, but curious. I wanted him to rest his head in my lap while I sat on the floor next to him and he told me all about her, and then I could kiss him and make it better. He was sitting back in his chair, legs clad in worn dark blue jeans spread slightly, foot tapping along, eyes intermittently lost in memory, in song, and there, present, with us. He was beautiful, and the crowd could tell he was someone to be silent for. He made me want to curl up next to him, on the ground, if need be, and I smiled in a way I don't seem to do all that often in New York City.

I'd tried to play it cool after the show, but I'd still stammered my way through greeting him. Pushing forty, you'd think I'd have a clue how to talk to a man—or in this case, man-boy— but that ability had forsaken me. Thankfully, Dean agreed to dinner the next night, telling me he loved greasy spoons. I couldn't remember the last time a guy had told a truth like that, rather than trying to impress me with the latest trendy boîte.

Over burgers dripping with grease and fries with even more,

we talked and talked and talked. The place is open twenty-four hours so they didn't care that we stayed from nine 'til three in the morning, as long as we kept ordering coffee. He reached for the bill and I noted the twenty-dollar tip he left, impressed. He offered me a ride home, and even though I usually walk or take the subway, I agreed, wanting to spend more time with him, as much as I could get. I'd expected him to pin me to his car, even though our conversation was more cerebral than flirty. We'd made out, for another hour, and his hands had gone up my shirt but he hadn't tried to get me to come home with him or to come home with me, just dropped me off like a gentleman. I soon discovered that's exactly what he was—a gentle man—and I'd been trying to make him a little less gentle as the weeks turned into months.

I knew he was busy with shows most nights and trying to woo record label A&R types the rest of the time, so I didn't push him. This was a weekend we'd set aside for ourselves, and instead of the hassle of going away, we'd settled on a staycation right at my apartment. Phones and computers off, our focus would be totally on each other, which I'd taken—or at least, hoped—to mean lots of blazing-hot sex. I'd gone to get waxed and while I usually leave a landing strip of hair in front, this time I told my waxer to take it all off. "Someone special going to see?" she asked.

Sometimes I get a little freaked out by too much conversation in the salon, but this time I was happy to wax on, if you will, about my new man. He was so sweet and sexy all in one, and I even gave her a postcard touting his next gig.

So as I'm sitting on his lap, I'm waiting for him to make his move, and then finally I just go for it. "Dean," I say, sitting up, looking him directly in the eye, blocking his view of the TV. "I want you. By which I mean, I want your cock. In my mouth, in my pussy, everywhere. I thought you'd have figured that out by now. I dream about you. I touch myself and think about you. Don't you want me?" I ask, noting a creeping edge of whiny neediness entering my voice.

"Oh, my god, of course I do. I can't believe you'd think otherwise." He pauses, and I settle into his lap again. He tries to look away, but I steer his gaze directly toward me. "Okay, I'm just gonna come right out and say this and if you don't want to see me after this I totally understand, but I hope you will. I've never done this before. I'm a virgin. And I'm worried that someone like you will be disappointed."

Whoa. I turn to look at him, but now his eyes are closed. I stroke his cheek tenderly, suddenly protective of him—not his virginity, which I very much plan to take, but his heart. I'd known right away this was "serious," but not until this moment exactly how serious. "Look at me. Open your eyes."

He does, his body trembling. "Dean, I want you—all of you. It's okay. I'm not expecting you to be like anyone but yourself. Do you understand that?"

He nods, but his eyes seem cloudy still, like he doesn't really get it. "Look, baby...do I want to sleep with you? I can't lie—yes, yes I do. Am I going to push you to do it sooner than you'd want to? Of course not. I want you, not some random cock. I want the whole package." I don't say that I'd had plenty of other more experienced packages, and here I was, forty and single, and so over the guys who were cocky enough to think they owned the world, or at least, New York City.

He stares at me for a long time, and finally a small smile appears on his face. "The whole thing? Are you sure you can handle it?" His laugh is soft, but definitely a laugh, as he takes my hand and presses it tight against his hardness. Then neither of us speaks, and the enormity of what we are about to do washes over me. If I weren't sure I wanted him—him, all of him, everything from his curls that seemed to melt through my fingers to the omnipresent stubble on his chin to the elaborate snake tattooed along his arm, every strum of his guitar and every brooding, beautiful look—I wouldn't keep touching him. There'd been times in my life when I would have "fucked like a man," as they say, taken what I could get, what I wanted, and then moved on. And while I desperately want him at that moment, his cock is just a part of what I want. I do want everything—I'm greedy like that—but I don't want it by any means necessary. I wouldn't want to use him for sex and move on, leaving him, shattered, to write a song or even an album about the bitch who broke his heart. I'm suddenly more hungry than horny, hungry for the look he is giving me, the heat that is penetrating through our clothes. If you can be hungry for a hint of forever, that's what I am.

But we are here, now, and I can't know what will happen, if I will break his heart or he mine. The best laid plans and all that, but still, I can't worry about every possible eventuality. You can live in fear forever and never walk outside your door, never take even a baby step into the unknown. If he's willing to take that first step with me, I'm ready, too. I know that when I stand and pull him up and toward my bedroom, I'm not doing so as some wise-woman courtesan intent on teaching a new young thing tricks he'll use on other women. I'm not trying to teach him anything, but simply to share myself with and indulge and love him, for as long as we are able to.

For a moment I wish I were a virgin again, too, and in a way, I am. This is new for me; the only other lover I've had who was a virgin was when I was one, too, way back when. And I've never been with someone who felt so right in a forever kind of way, someone who's made me slow down enough to savor the moment. We walk into my room and we tangle around each other, rolling around on the bed until I'm on top of him, pressing myself urgently against him. "Shouldn't I be on top?" he asks when I start to slither out of my dress.

"If you want to, but there are no 'shoulds' with sex," I say, as I undo my bra, letting my breasts spring free. "Whatever you've heard, forget about it. Focus on me," I tell him, then lean down and kiss him. "I'll take care of you. I promise."

I take that promise seriously as I lean down and gently kiss his neck, forcing myself to slow down as much as I possibly can, to make sure his first time is not a blur, but a blessing. I nuzzle my face against his neck, then his chest, then kiss the snake around his arm, trailing my tongue down his inner arm until I get to his fingers. I suck each one gently, then more firmly, while my hand plays with his cock through his jeans, until I can't wait any longer, and undo the zipper. I've felt him through his clothes before, and certainly have pictured Dean's dick plenty of times, but that's nothing compared to what it feels like in my hand, hot and hard and mine. Knowing I'm his first makes it all the hotter as I listen to his intakes of breath, his murmurs, as I simply hold him in my hand. I want to do so many things all at once, but I force myself not to race ahead; we have, I hope, a lifetime to explore each other's bodies.

He doesn't ask if I like it, but I can tell he wants to know from the look on his face, nervous, expectant, hopeful. I want to say, "It's beautiful," but I don't want him to take that the wrong way, so instead I simply smile and lean down to kiss it, starting at the base, then working my way up. I press my lips against his heat, and it's almost like I'm the virgin here. No, not exactly—there is a familiarity to his hardness—but there is so much newness I find myself marveling at what he is giving me, what we are sharing. My frantic urge to have him inside me has given way to something more tender and sweet, less a desire to possess him than to prolong our mutual pleasure.

I lick around his balls, then up his shaft, then taste the head, attuned to every cue and response from Dean. I like having him at my mercy, but I don't want to torture him—too much, anyway. "Turn over," I say softly, and he does, unquestioning. I massage his ass; his firm, round, tight ass. He jogs when he needs a break from playing, and his body is strong because of it, but he's not a showoff type. He is simply young and able to easily stay in shape, and I show him how much I like that about him, how much I want to devour every inch of him. I massage his buttcheeks until I can't wait any longer, then lick along the edge of his hole, then plunge inside. He squirms and moans and I know he wasn't expecting this. Then I trace my thumb around the wet area, and reach for some lube. I wasn't planning on this either, but one of the first rules of sex, at least in my play-book, is to expect the unexpected, and I want to make sure he knows that's what I'm looking for more than any kind of sexual prowess or talent. I want us to have adventures I couldn't have dreamed of before him.

And then he is opening up to me, letting my index finger in, his muffled moans audible through the pillow. I can already envision using something more here, strapping on a dildo, playing around with gender, playing around with each other. *Play*, I think, as I press deeper. That's what's been missing from my life pre-Dean; not the kind exhibited by men known as players, but by real men, or rather, the only one I need. I want Dean to play me like he does his guitar, plucking me, pinching me, making sweet music. Even if we play that same song over and over, it will always sound slightly different. I smile as my finger gets him off, and keep smiling as I wash off and we take a hot, bubbly bath that turns into me climbing on top of him and our bodies joining, wet and slippery and passionate. I slither against him and he holds me tight. As I come, falling against him, my laugh ringing in the air, I feel high on this feeling he's given me. I don't know if I'll be able to explain it to Dean, but I see now that I've been just as much a virgin as he's been. This is what I've been missing, right here, and it's about much more than how hard and hot his cock is for me. It's about all of it together, the love wrapped around the lust placed inside the huge heart this sweet, sexy man is offering me. I look forward to serenading him with the sound of my desire and learning right along with him.

# ABOUT THE
# AUTHORS

**TENILLE BROWN** is a Southern, shoe-shopping, wine-drinking writer whose erotic fiction has been published online and in over thirty print anthologies including *Ultimate Lesbian Erotica 2007, Fast Girls, Making the Hook Up, Iridescence, F Is for Fetish* and *Best Bondage Erotica 2011*. She blogs at thesteppingstone.blogspot.com.

EPIC award winner **ANGELA CAPERTON** writes eclectic erotica that challenges genre conventions. Look for her stories published with Black Lace and eBury Publishing, Cleis, Circlet, Coming Together, Drollerie, eXtasy Books, and in the indie magazine *Out of the Gutter*. Visit her at blog.angelacaperton.com.

**CASSANDRA CARR** lives in Western New York with her husband, Inspiration, and daughter, Too Cute for Words. Her debut novel is titled *Talk to Me*. For more information about Cassandra, see her website booksbycassandracarr.com.

**ELIZABETH COLDWELL** lives and writes in London. Her stories have appeared in numerous anthologies including *Do Not Disturb*, *The Mile High Club* and *Obsessed*. She can be found at The (Really) Naughty Corner, elizabethcoldwell.wordpress.com, when she's not whipping up something tasty in the kitchen.

**KATE DOMINIC** is a former technical writer who now writes about much more interesting ways to connect Tab *A* with Slot *B* (or *C* or *D*). She is the author of over three hundred short love stories and is currently deep in the research phase of a steamy romance novel.

**JEREMY EDWARDS** is the author of the erotocomedic novel *Rock My Socks Off* and the erotic story collection *Spark My Moment*. His work has appeared in over fifty anthologies, including *The Mammoth Book of Best New Erotica, vols. 7–9*. Readers can drop in on him at jeremyedwardserotica.com.

**MICHAEL A. GONZALES** has written erotica that has appeared in *Brown Sugar 2*, *Gotta Have It: 69 Stories of Sudden Sex* and *Best Sex Writing 2005*. In addition, Gonzales has penned cover stories for *Stella*, *Essence*, *Vibe* and *Uptown*. He lives in Brooklyn.

**K D GRACE** lives in England with her husband. She is passionate about nature, writing, and sex—not necessarily in that order. She enjoys long distance walking and extreme vegetable gardening. Along with numerous short stories, she has published two novels, *The Initiation of Ms. Holly* and *The Pet Shop*.

**ABIGAIL GREY** has enjoyed writing ever since creating a series about friends while in junior high. This is her first piece submitted for publication, bringing a childhood dream to life. She lives in Michigan, battling for computer time with her online-gamer family.

**SKYLAR KADE** currently resides in sunny Southern California, alternately cursing the polluted air and adoring the often-perfect weather. She spends her time asking the cabana boys to bring her more mimosas and feed her strawberries while she dreams up her next naughty adventure. Find her at skylarkade.com.

**LOLITA LOPEZ** writes deliciously naughty romantic and erotic tales in a wide variety of flavors. She lives in Texas with her husband, daughter and one seriously goofy Great Dane. You can find Lo's latest news and releases at lolitalopez.com.

**HANNA MARTINE** writes contemporary and paranormal romance. She has two novels forthcoming from Berkley Sensation Trade. Visit her at hannamartine.com.

**CATHERINE PAULSSEN,** thirty-three, has lived in England, Israel and Germany. She loves Motown music, meeting her friends at her favorite coffee place or sitting there by herself to read and enjoy people-watching. She works as a freelancer in Berlin; whenever she has the time, she writes erotica.

Eroticist **GISELLE RENARDE** (wix.com/gisellerenarde/erotica) is a queer Canadian, contributor to dozens of short-story anthologies, an avid volunteer, and author of numerous electronic and print books.

**DONNA GEORGE STOREY** is the author of *Amorous Woman,* a steamy novel about an American woman's love affair with

Japan. Her short fiction has appeared in numerous journals and anthologies including *Passion: Erotic Romance for Women, Obsessed, Penthouse* and *Best Women's Erotica*. Read more of her work at DonnaGeorgeStorey.com.

**ALYSSA TURNER's** writings address a woman's desire to really have it all—including the things she's not supposed to want. Her publishing credits include "Two For One" in *Best Women's Erotica 2011*, edited by Violet Blue; and novellas *Send* and *Bittersweet*.

**ANNA WATSON** lives and writes near Boston. She is married to the butch of her dreams, and they share the house with two lovely sons, a feisty Cairn terrier boy, and two grandma kitties. For more of her work, see *Sometimes She Lets Me*, Justus Roux's *Erotic Tales 2, Girl Crazy* and *Take Me There*.

**VERONICA WILDE** is an erotic romance author whose books have been published with Liquid Silver Books and Samhain Publishing. Please visit her at veronicawilde.com.

**KRISTINA WRIGHT** (kristinawright.com) is an author and the editor of the Cleis Press anthologies *Fairy Tale Lust, Dream Lover, Steamlust* and *Best Erotic Romance 2012*. Her erotica has appeared in over eighty anthologies. She lives in Virginia with her family and spends a great deal of time writing in coffee shops.

# ABOUT
# THE EDITOR

**RACHEL KRAMER BUSSEL** (rachelkramerbussel.com) is a
New York–based author, editor and blogger. She has edited
over forty books of erotica, including *Anything for You; Suite
Encounters; Going Down; Irresistible; Best Bondage Erotica
2011, 2012 and 2013; Gotta Have It; Obsessed; Women in
Lust; Her Surrender; Orgasmic; Bottoms Up: Spanking Good
Stories; Spanked: Red-Cheeked Erotica; Naughty Spanking
Stories from A to Z 1 and 2; Fast Girls; Smooth; Passion;
The Mile High Club; Do Not Disturb; Going Down; Tasting
Him; Tasting Her; Please, Sir; Please, Ma'am; He's on Top;
She's on Top; Caught Looking; Hide and Seek; Crossdressing;
Rubber Sex; Anything for You* and *Suite Encounters*. She is
*Best Sex Writing* series editor, and winner of 8 IPPY (Independ-
ent Publisher) Awards. Her work has been published in over
one hundred anthologies, including *Best American Erotica
2004 and 2006; Zane's Chocolate Flava 2* and *Purple Panties;
Everything You Know About Sex Is Wrong; Single State of the*

*Union* and *Desire: Women Write About Wanting.* She wrote
the popular "Lusty Lady" column for the *Village Voice.*
     Rachel has written for *AVN, Bust,* Cleansheets.com, *Cosmo-
politan, Curve,* The Daily Beast, Fresh Yarn, TheFrisky.com,
*Glamour,* Gothamist, Huffington Post, *Inked,* Mediabistro,
*Newsday, New York Post, Penthouse, Playgirl, Radar,* The
Root, Salon, *San Francisco Chronicle, Time Out New York*
and *Zink,* among others. She has appeared on "The Gayle
King Show," "The Martha Stewart Show," "The Berman and
Berman Show," NY1 and Showtime's "Family Business." She
hosted the popular In the Flesh Erotic Reading Series (inthefle-
shreadingseries.com), featuring readers from Susie Bright to
Zane, and speaks at conferences, does readings and teaches
erotic writing workshops across the country. She blogs at
lustylady.blogspot.com.

# More from Rachel Kramer Bussel

**Buy 4 books,**
**Get 1** *FREE*\*

**Do Not Disturb**
*Hotel Sex Stories*
Edited by Rachel Kramer Bussel

A delicious array of hotel hookups where it seems like anything can happen—and quite often does. "If *Do Not Disturb* were a hotel, it would be a 5-star hotel with the luxury of 24/7 entertainment available."—Erotica Revealed
978-1-57344-344-9 $14.95

---

**Bottoms Up**
*Spanking Good Stories*
Edited by Rachel Kramer Bussel

As sweet as it is kinky, *Bottoms Up* will propel you to pick up a paddle and share in both pleasure and pain, or perhaps simply turn the other cheek.
ISBN 978-1-57344-362-3 $14.95

**Orgasmic**
*Erotica for Women*
Edited by Rachel Kramer Bussel

What gets you off? Let *Orgasmic* count the ways...with 25 stories focused on female orgasm, there is something here for every reader.
ISBN 978-1-57344-402-6 $14.95

**Please, Sir**
*Erotic Stories of Female Submission*
Edited by Rachel Kramer Bussel

These 22 kinky stories celebrate the thrill of submission by women who know exactly what they want.
ISBN 978-1-57344-389-0 $14.95

**Fast Girls**
*Erotica for Women*
Edited by Rachel Kramer Bussel

*Fast Girls* celebrates the girl with a reputation, the girl who goes all the way, and the girl who doesn't know how to say "no."
ISBN 978-1-57344-384-5 $14.95

\* Free book of equal or lesser value. Shipping and applicable sales tax extra.
Cleis Press • (800) 780-2279 • orders@cleispress.com
www.cleispress.com

# Many More Than Fifty Shades of Erotica

Buy 4 books, Get 1 FREE*

**Please, Sir**
*Erotic Stories of Female Submission*
Edited by Rachel Kramer Bussel

If you liked *Fifty Shades of Grey,* you'll love the explosive stories of *Yes, Sir.* These damsels delight in the pleasures of taking risks to be rewarded by the men who know their deepest desires. Find out why nothing is as hot as the power of the words "Please, Sir."
ISBN 978-1-57344-389-0 $14.95

---

**Yes, Sir**
*Erotic Stories of Female Submission*
Edited by Rachel Kramer Bussel

Bound, gagged or spanked—or controlled with just a glance—these lucky women experience the breathtaking thrills of sexual submission. *Yes, Sir* shows that pleasure is best when dispensed by a firm hand.
ISBN 978-1-57344-310-4 $15.95

**He's on Top**
*Erotic Stories of Male Dominance and Female Submission*
Edited by Rachel Kramer Bussel

As true tops, the bossy hunks in these stories understand that BDSM is about exulting in power that is freely yielded. These kinky stories celebrate women who know exactly what they want.
ISBN 978-1-57344-270-1 $14.95

**Best Bondage Erotica 2012**
Edited by Rachel Kramer Bussel

How do you want to be teased, tied and tantalized? Whether you prefer a tough top with shiny handcuffs, the tug of rope on your skin or the sound of your lover's command, Rachel Kramer Bussel serves your needs.
ISBN 978-1-57344-754-6 $15.95

**Bottoms Up**
*Spanking Good Stories*
Edited by Rachel Kramer Bussel

As sweet as it is kinky, *Bottoms Up* will propel you to pick up a paddle and share in both pleasure and pain, or perhaps simply turn the other cheek. This torrid tour de force is essential reading.
ISBN 978-1-57344-362-3 $15.95

---

* Free book of equal or lesser value. Shipping and applicable sales tax extra.
Cleis Press • (800) 780-2279 • orders@cleispress.com
www.cleispress.com